ONE
WITH
BIRD

ONE WITH BIRD

And Other Stories

douglas k german

ONE WITH BIRD
AND OTHER STORIES

iUniverse books may be ordered through booksellers or by contacting:

*iUniverse
1663 Liberty Drive
Bloomington, IN 47403
www.iuniverse.com
1-800-Authors (1-800-288-4677)*

*ISBN: 978-1-5320-3520-3 (sc)
ISBN: 978-1-5320-3521-0 (e)*

Library of Congress Control Number: 2017916848

Print information available on the last page.

iUniverse rev. date: 11/09/2017

It is not possible to take twenty-six tiny symbols, no matter how arranged, and explain what was, what is, or what will be.

—dkg

Table of Contents

One with Bird

Saturday, October 8, 1938

Max draws the shade against the crimson sun, straightens the chairs around the conference table, and checks the schedule tacked to the rolltop desk. *The Schmidt funeral today, one on Friday—hey, not bad for a small town out on the prairie.*

As he turns to go to the back room to work on the stiff for Friday, he hears the anteroom door open. *Awfully early.* It is someone old: sounds of a struggle, huffing and puffing, the clank of a cane. Max, tall, thin as a string bean, dressed in a black vested suit, peeks through the crack of the open door as he straightens his tie, slicks his hair, and prepares to go out to greet the visitor, to help whoever it is with the wind blowing the door. *My God, it's William, ol' man Schmidt's brother, the mean, cranky one.* Max steps back so as to not be seen and lets William make his way back, back to view his brother's body. *Hell, everyone knows they haven't shared a word in years.* Max smiles to himself. *Now this should be something. Best stay out of it for damned sure.* William—rotund, dressed as the gentleman farmer he is, sporting a hand-painted tie and a gaudy diamond ring—struggles on in.

Max stays in his office until William, stooped like he's looking for loose change, has made his way to the side of his brother's coffin, then softly moves nearby out of view to assist if needed, to observe. William has hooked his cane on the side of the coffin and with trembling, gnarled hands breaks off a red rose from one of the floral arrangements adorning the casket, causing the stand and flowers to crash to the floor. William stares at the flowers on the floor for a moment and then turns back. He picks up his brother's hand and puts the rose in it. He kisses the hand, stares into his brother's rouged face for a moment, then fumbles for his cane and turns to go.

Max steps back farther out of view and waits for William to toddle by and out. William grunts and canes past as if in a world of his own. Then, as he makes his way to the door, in a voice as even, as strong, as cold as a pump handle on a frosty morning, he says, "Max, if you let anyone know I loved my brother, I'll kill ya." As he steps on out, Max hears him say over the wind, "The son of a bitch was always the favorite."

Ruby scrubs the egg from the skillet and pumps some water to rinse it. *What a wonder and a great big thunder,*

ol' Roanie finally lay down. She shakes her head, recalling her time at home. *That cow never got its fill.* Ruby sighs, and a light passes over her round face, a cheeky face with batty eyelashes, mouth and lips of a pouty child, black hair in a bob. She can hear her father tell her to go get the cows in, but not before the last one lies down, full, chewing its cud. Only then could she bring the cows in to be milked, go to her place where it felt she was underwater, not a thing, just a deep hum, where animals sang and her wand melted rocks into music. That big roan watched her out of one eye and grazed with a smirk until it choked, as if it knew she wanted to go play.

She moons as she hangs up the black iron skillet, wipes off the cob stove. And then—childlike, palms on the counter, shoulders hunched, a foot toed and swinging back and forth—she wistfully gazes out the kitchen window across the Platte Valley toward the river. The giant egg yolk rising in the east has torched the barn into a bonfire with doors. A shadow looms through the fire like a monster on a movie screen. Ruby straightens and takes a deep breath as she watches her hubby, Aksel, drive out in his brand-new '38 Ford, headed to town with Anton, their oldest. That could only mean little Carsten was again outside bawling like to scare the horses. She turns back to what she was doing.

The church called earlier. *Looking for a saint and my famous lemon pie. Devil's cake for the Schmidt funeral will do him.* Ruby smiles and tosses the tea towel in the air as she opens the icebox to get out eggs and milk, whiffs of breakfast still in the air. She swings the icebox door shut with her foot, hands full with eggs and milk, and pulls the breadboard out with a finger. *I'll pop a cake into the oven and get prissied up for the funeral. Gotta drop Carsten off at the Beenies' on the way.*

With the cake finally in the oven, Ruby puts the eggs and milk back in the icebox and closes the flour bin, glancing out the sink window to check on Carsten playing in the leaves. *Smartest kid I could hope to have, for sure the ugly duckling.* Lips pursed, she shakes her head, heaves a sigh, puts everything aside. She hangs on the sill, head against the cool glass, watching Carsten in the yard just as he picks up Anton's cat by its tail. She knocks on the window and, with head cocked to one side and a face that says, *You know better*, wags a finger like a metronome set for a dirge. Big eared, bucktoothed, with stringy blond hair and cheeks of a cherub, Carsten grins and waves with a flutter of the fingers. Ruby smiles back and heads to the bedroom to ready herself. The cake should be done by the time she's ready.

Her nails not yet dry, she works the sacred drawer open with thumb and finger as if moving a hot pan. Sacred with objects of lust: a scarlet scarf that goes with her black dress, a pair of silk stockings with only a slight run that can be stopped with clear nail polish, a silky slip Aksel got her for Christmas, straight out of Sears & Roebuck all the way from Chicago, and a naughty negligee for Saturday nights, some Sheik condoms, and a douche bag.

She plucks out the slip and hips the drawer closed, blowing her nails to make sure they are dry. She puts the slip over her bobbed hair and slithers it down her long-necked, willowy body. Looking around as if someone might be watching, she hikes the slip and strikes a pose like she sees in the movie magazines at the hairdresser, smiles, and blows bubbles off the palm of her hand. *God, I love Aksel so. I wish he were here right now. Phew, I gotta get ready. So like his father when it comes to the urge.* She moans, fingering perfume on the nuzzle-and-bite curve of her neck.

Ruby smiles as she finishes dressing and recalls how Mr. Schmidt, may he rest in peace, was complaining one day in the drugstore about how he could only sire daughters, six of them. Aksel's father, who happened to be there and who had eight boys and seven daughters, suggested Mr. Schmidt hold his chin up at the magic moment if he desired a boy, chin down for another girl. *But he never sprung a boy ... Never mind the chin now, Mr. Schmidt—it's toooes zup!* Ruby giggles to herself as she pins on her hat, smooths her black Sunday dress, checking for lint. Then she grabs her coat and purse and yells at Carsten to get in the car.

"Damned trucks." Ruby checks the rearview mirror. "Sorry, Carsten. Sit back now. I meant to say silly trucks, okay?" Carsten puts the fingers of one hand over his mouth like the monkey who speaks no evil and wags a finger of the other hand ... just-like-a-me-tro-nome-set-for-a-dirge. Ruby rolls her eyes as if to say, *Oops*, checks the rearview mirror again, double clutches, shifts to second, and pumps the brake as she waits for the dust from the truck to clear before turning into Gramma Beenblossom's drive.

She honks at the Rhode Island Reds, swerves to avoid the Irish setter bounding out into the yard, just missing the big cottonwood by the picket gate, before skidding to a halt, holding Carsten back from hitting the dash with her free arm. The dust rolls over the car and into the trees like a mist lifting off a lake into the forest. *Now that, by God, is how to arrive. No one needs to wonder if you're here. I'm late.* She lays on the horn and piles out as if she has run over somebody, goes around to the other side to get Carsten out, and heads to the door, Carsten in tow.

Gramma Beenblossom is working her way out the door: tiny and bony, in a bandana head scarf and her chore clothes sewn of flour sacks, a milk pail hanging at her elbow. Stiff-necked, she turns with minced steps at the ruckus, looks over her glasses at Carsten and then, with a resigned, knowing smile, up to Ruby.

"There's Grammie Beenie, Carsten," Ruby encourages as she holds the gate open. Then she does as mothers do—assures Carsten he'll have fun, she'll be back soon—caught between being afraid something might happen and relieved to be free for a while. "You be good now, won't you?" And then she thanks Gramma Beenie for taking care of Carsten as she gives her a peck on the cheek and explains she's late, must be off. Gramma Beenie and Carsten walk out to the car with Ruby, making small talk, easing the going away of Mom—Carsten trying to hold on, Mom trying to get away. And then Ruby is off.

Ruby shifts to high, hitches herself up straight with the steering wheel, looks in the rearview mirror to check her lipstick, and recalls the first time Aksel took her down to meet the Beenblossoms, just neighbors, not really related. When they pulled into the yard, she thought they were in the Ozarks. The Beenblossoms were standing out by a rickety old barn, no paint, doors sagging. Just finished milking. Dogs aplenty. Chickens all over. Junk cars back in the windbreak. Weeds. Huge garden. And she was supposed to leave her kids there.

Ruby smiles as she remembers how, as they were getting out of the car, Aksel squeezed her knee and said, "Be nice." The Beenblossoms invited them in. Mr. Beenblossom offered them each a straight-backed chair at the kitchen table and sat down in his spot by the potbellied stove after stoking it, adding some cobs, and adjusting the vent. Then he began to roll a cigarette while the missus started a kettle of water. Everything was so humble— simple, bare, yet warm. The smells of bacon, kerosene, cobs, smoke, and candles. Ruby felt as if things had stopped and this was it—why go on? Aksel carried on as if he were family. Ruby just took it all in, thinking, *And I'm a fifth cousin to John Adams.* Mr. Beenblossom—Beenie, as Ruby calls him now—sat back, ran his fingers through his thin, stringy, yellowish-gray hair. He sighed as if to gather himself, stared across the room, reaching into his bibs for his Bull Durham. He broke the blue tax seal, untangled the red strings. Then he turned to Aksel as he fished for his papers in his bibs with a bony, blue-veined hand as knotted as an oak stick. *I couldn't take my eyes off him,* Ruby remembers. "Aksel," he said, clicking his false teeth, finally finding the papers, "how're those boys a yurs doin'? Hardly see ya go by with Carsten." He held his index finger in the paper to hold it open, tapping the bag of tobacco, pulled the string tight with his teeth, put the bag back in his bibs, licked the paper, and rolled it, twisting the ends. *Does he see it too?* Ruby remembers thinking.

As he struck a match on the bottom of his chair and took a draw, blowing the match out, Aksel, with his elbows on his knees, looked down at the floor, then back up at Mr. Beenblossom, but didn't say a thing. Just then Mrs. Beenblossom sat a chipped plate on the green-and-white plaid oilcloth and a speckled blue enamel cup for each of them. Ruby smiles and shakes her head in disbelief as she heads for town. *Postum, and saltine crackers spread with lard, sprinkled with salt.*

Carsten squats down at Gramma Beenie's feet, holds his hand out to the chickens, talking to them as if they were kittens, trying to get them to come over to him. Gramma Beenie, milk pail still hanging at her elbow, snugs her head scarf. "C'mon, Carsten. Let's go see what Grandpa's doin' in the barn," she says, groping for his hand. "Maybe Grandpa needs yur help?"

As Gramma Beenie nears the barn, with Carsten lagging behind, gawking around, kicking at clods, she hears the rhythmic, singsong bizz-buzz of milk cutting into the foam of a near-full bucket, the cow shifting in the stanchion, and Grandpa gently talking to it. "Sooo, boss, we're near done." The smell of sour manure, sweet hay, steaming cows, and Bag Balm waft from the barn. She hangs on the dutch door, her chin resting on top, and looks in at the two, Beenie and the cow. Carsten tries to jump up to see in too, whining, hitting her out of frustration. She puts her hand back to fend him off and asks, "Whatcha got for Carsten to do?" Silence—except for the bizz-buzz and the muffled chomping of hay.

"Well, I s'pose he could help clean out the henhouse.

Maybe go with me to fence down t'other end of the pasture." More bizz-buzz, chomping, and a hanging silence, as both seem to be thinking, maybe waiting for a sense of the moment—what thoughts to voice, what misgivings to share, what risks to run, what spell to break. She looks down between her arms at Carsten, who is between her and the barn door, looking up at her. She waits.

Finally Beenie says, "But ya know, he doesn't much like to be outside, get dirty. Maybe ya have him do something in the house—seems he likes that. Ya know whadda mean, don'tcha?"

She doesn't say anything, turns and looks out across the yard, off into the distance toward the river, the hills, wondering whether she should pick up on his insinuation. Then she turns back and, while looking down at Carsten, says, "Yeah, I know whatcha mean."

There are no words between them for a long time as he milks and she stands there stroking Carsten's hair back, looking into his eyes. "Yeah, the last time he sewed, helped me with the cooking, and played with the Kewpie dolls," she finally says with a heave and a sigh. "His hands are like those of a girl." There is just the bizz-buzz of milking. Finally she sets the bucket down and heads to the house with Carsten, talking about the things they could do, Carsten as excited as a kid about to get to go to town.

From a distance Ruby can see parked cars for several blocks and people crossing the avenue arched with elms. *It's one of those big ones,* Ruby silently mouths as she pulls along the curb behind the last car, glancing at the license plate to gauge who is showing up. *The Godfreys, 18-20—they've had that number since license plates were first issued. Strange they'd be here. Always wanted the same pieces of ground.* She checks her lipstick in the rearview mirror again, swings her legs out, skirt hiked up, just as a carload of high school boys passes. They lay on the horn and whistle. She can't keep from smiling while acting like she doesn't see them. Her bobbed hair, fast driving, bright-red lipstick, and short skirts—bit of a flapper look, now passé in New York City but hanging on out here—have earned her glances of scorn, smirks of envy in this backwater town on Lincoln Highway three hundred miles west of Omaha.

Ruby spots Lena waiting in the dark line of mourners on the granite steps up to the entrance of the grandest church in town, the bricked First Methodist Church. Tall and big-boned, horsey faced, with a dolled-up, big hairdo, and dressed in the latest from Omaha, flashy jewelry and a mink stole. One by one the mourners disappear inside after a long wait, the men doffing their hats, the women going first. Drawing attention, responding with an appropriate show of solemnness, Ruby nods to acquaintances and friends. And then as she makes her way to Lena, Ruby breaks into a smile that says, *Here we go again.* Lena, ever the dramatic, glamorous if not beautiful, feigns greeting a long-lost friend with open arms. Her trademark husky voice, and a full and sinuous mouth to go with it, erupts over the whispered conversations by others. They hug and carry on, and then Ruby, noticing the looks of those around them, tries to hush Lena yet can't keep from giggling herself.

Continuing to carry on—with Lena talking and laughing as if at a party, as if she didn't know it was a funeral, Ruby giggling and hushing her—they make their way in line step by step up toward the entrance. Lena is a step ahead of Ruby, her back to the doorway. Those in front and back of them in line stop their muffled conversations, some turning grim as if to show their disapproval, others apparently hoping to hear what's being said, and others, with eyes dancing, looking off into the distance, unable to suppress a smile.

While continuing to talk, Lena glances over her shoulder to check their progress and then turns back to Ruby. "What in the hell is taking so long? The body'll rot before we get in," Lena says in a whisper intended to be heard by those nearby. She takes one of the last steps up, then turns back to Ruby. Ruby flinches, hunches her shoulders as if to hide, shushes Lena, and begins to giggle as they reach the entrance. Lena turns around to go in, Ruby close behind with a hand on her back having nudged her to let her know it was their turn to enter from bright sun to near darkness.

"Ahhhh! Oh my God!" Lena belts out, hands flying up in fear, as she backs into Ruby and nearly knocks her down. There, right inside, around the corner, is the open casket. Lena has bumped into it right near the dead man's face. "Christ!" Lena exclaims with a mix of anger and embarrassment. They quickly gather themselves, Ruby calming Lena, and then both start to giggle, hushing each other, and hustle into the sanctuary to be seated, trying to regain composure. They are seated as the organ player sets the mood with the somber tones of "We Shall Gather at the River," accompanied by the essences of hymnals, colognes, mothballs, candles, and formaldehyde.

The pastor stands to move to the pulpit. Ruby and Lena look up with pious faces, strained from suppressed giggles and snorts, shoulders heaving as if crying. Ruby finds her hankie to wipe the tears from her eyes. The pastor begins the opening prayer. With heads bowed, both desperately trying to not laugh, Lena leans over to Ruby to try to say something but can't without laughing, unable to even whisper. They both go off in a shoulder-shaking snigger, trying not to let go with a snort, trying desperately to regain the composure fitting to their husbands' stature in the community. Finally, as the pastor reads the obituary, both are nearly composed. Ruby leans over to Lena and says with a strained calmness, "We—" She suppresses a laugh and starts again, squeezing out the words. "We-have-got-to"—she takes a deep breath to compose herself—"stop … People-will-think"—another deep breath and a near snort—"we are taking this too hard … like-we-were"—deep breath—"doingtheoldgoat." And off they were again, heads bowed, shoulders shaking.

Lost in thought, the roar of the plane's engine masking the sounds and a sense of the rest of the world, Aksel gazes out over the great Platte Valley, a valley squared off in 640-acre sections by roads disappearing into the hills and over the horizon, a valley laced with irrigation canals worming their way through the rich, loamy soils to thirsty fields of corn, a valley belonging to a river claimed to be a mile wide and an inch deep, a valley where Aksel was born and has made his way in spite of depressed commodity prices and the unusually dry weather. He wonders why he is there, ponders what is beyond. He looks over at Anton, who has his nose pressed against the window, peering down. Aksel smiles as he contemplates his son, then gets ready to give Anton a thrill.

After checking Anton's seat belt, Aksel pulls the carburetor heat on, makes clearance turns to the left and the right to look for other aircraft, eases the throttle back, and raises the nose, watching the airspeed drop, centering the ball in the turn coordinator, waiting for the stall. *Stick forward, opposite rudder, ease stick back.* All goes quiet except for the idling engine. The plane shudders; he kicks left rudder. The plane whips to the left, then spins violently straight down, the earth swirling below once, twice. Then he pushes the stick forward and gives right rudder, eases back on the stick to level flight again, pushes off the carburetor heat, and inches the throttle back in, the rush of air and engine noise filling the cabin. Aksel checks all the instruments, gets comfortable in his seat again, and, with his trademark smirk-grin that beams confidence, looks over to Anton.

Anton is still scrunched down in his seat unable to gain his breath, holding his stomach, a look of terror and glee on his face. He finally sits up, wipes the tears from his face from squinting so hard, and is able to muster in a voice still shaken, "Whoa, Dad, let's do that again!"

They head back to the airport and land. Aksel gives right rudder, some brake, and a burst of power to kick the tail of the silver, maroon-trimmed Luscombe around square with the tie-downs. He cuts the fuel mixture, turns the magnetos off, and flips open his seat belt as the prop flutters to a stop, the gyros still humming. He turns to Anton, who has his gaze locked on the instruments, as if wanting to touch them but daring not.

"How'd you like that?"

"I really like it when we do spins," Anton says, eyes shining. "Next time I want to do a loop."

Aksel grins with pride at his eight-year-old son, the son he always hoped for, a son who likes to do spins, a son like him. Yes, a handsome, quick, athletic son, a son beautiful, with a winsome smile, a head of dark, wavy hair, and the markings of the man he will one day be. They hop out, and Aksel ties down. Anton helps by chocking the wheels. He skins his knuckle but says nothing. Aksel notices, pleased.

Aksel dusts off his khakis, doffs his fedora, palming his graying hair back, dons the hat cocked to one side, and, with a hand on the hip, heads for the new Ford, striding with the confidence, the air of a successful young farmer—as handsome, as athletic as his favorite son. "Well, what do you say we go have something to eat downtown? Your mother's at a funeral."

Aksel puts his billfold away after paying the bill for the blue-plate specials at the Flock Inn Café and steps out into the brisk October sun, Anton holding the door for him. He acknowledges the looks, nods, and greetings of passersby on the sidewalk, then checks his watch as he and Anton head for the gleaming black Ford Fordor. *A little after one. Game three of the World Series will be starting soon.* "Anton, let's go check how Georg is doing raking hay and listen to the World Series."

Anton, a few steps ahead, snaps his head around to see whether his dad is serious. "Yeah, let's do that. I hope the Yankees win."

Aksel studies Anton as they walk along and grins a wistful grin that says, *Cheering for the favorites, eh?* "I'm betting on the Cubs, the underdogs," Aksel says as they climb in the car. He backs out and heads for the place south of the Platte River.

They pull into the field of fifth-cutting alfalfa, mowed, the sweet smell of drying hay heavy in the air. On the far end of the field Georg, Aksel's teenage brother, is on the F-20 tractor pulling the side-delivery rake. Aksel eases along the end of the field until he reaches the last windrow and then heads toward the tractor and rake. As Aksel approaches, Georg idles down, stops, slips the tractor out of gear, sets the brake, and swings down stiff legged. Tall and gangly, in blue bibs and no shirt, covered with hay leaves, he waits with a country-boy grin, his white teeth gleaming from a face caked in dust. Aksel pulls up, waits for the dust to drift off, and then rolls down the window. Anton leans over to see Georg, who dusts himself off as he approaches the car.

"Unhook the rake and pull the tractor up out of the way," Aksel tells Georg, grinning as if to say, *Watch this.* Georg looks confused for a moment and then nods and heads back to the tractor. Aksel swings the car around ready to pull in front of the rake. When Georg has the tractor out of the way, Aksel backs up to the tongue of the rake, steps out, and strides to the rear of the car. Anton hops out the other side.

"Georg, grab the log chain off the tractor," Aksel says, raising his chin to point. Georg gets the chain and then watches as Aksel hooks the rake to the car bumper. Aksel looks up at Georg with a grin as he finishes the hitch and can see that his brother seems amused but maybe too intimidated to say anything, acting like it is normal to hitch a rake to a new car. Georg steals a look at Anton. Anton is watching his dad with a very serious look on his face, as if wondering whether something is wrong, but then breaks into a faint smile. Aksel stands up, swipes his hands a couple of times, and says, grinning at the two as he heads to get back in the car, "Take me out to the ball game, boys … Get in."

They rake hay, Anton in back, Georg in the passenger seat, Aksel with his elbow out the window, glancing in the rearview to check how the clattering rake is going, the radio on. "… third ball game of a surprising Series. The Cubs here by the slimmest of margins, only beating Pittsburg 6–5 in the ninth for the pennant. The Yankees, on the other hand, here for the third year in a row with the likes of DiMaggio, Dickey, and Gehrig. The Cubs, meanwhile, pinning their hopes on Galan and Collins, their recent acquisition Dizzy Dean out with a toe injury. It's almost …"

Georg sneaks a look back at Anton, as if wanting to share his giddiness, and Aksel smiles at the exchange. Seeing Aksel's smile, Georg hesitates, flickers a smile of his own, sits up straight, puts one arm out the window, the other on the back of the seat, and shouts, "Go Yanks! Go Gehrig!"

And Anton yells, "Go Yanks! Go Gehrig!" then looks at his dad to see whether it is okay to yell. They rake, they listen, they yell.

The funeral over, calm regained, Ruby and Lena take refuge at Lena's home, one of the better in town, high-end, beyond her and her husband's means but worth it. Seated on an elegant footstool, elbow on her crossed knees, unwittingly striking the pose of a pinup girl, Ruby swirls her highball, staring out the picture window. "My God, Lena, we may be done in this town."

"Oh, Ruby, they'll get over it," Lena shouts from the kitchen. She emerges with some tidbits and says, "Did you see the look on the pastor's face? My Lord, I thought he was going to descend upon us with the wrath of heaven and hell combined." They both start to giggle again, Ruby waving her hand, bracelet jingling, as if to say, *Please, please, no more.* Then they sit quietly, thinking, sipping their drinks, moving to other thoughts.

"What you thinking, Ruby?"

Ruby looks into her drink, then looks to Lena with eyes brimming with tears and a forced smile, caught between wanting to share and thinking she shouldn't. She wipes the tears away with the back of her hand, takes a deep breath, and blows it out to gain composure, fumbling to find her hankie hidden in her bosom. "Carsten ... Aksel ..." She sniffs and runs a hand through her hair. "I'm pregnant."

"Oh Lord," Lena says and then catches herself. "But

that's wonderful … isn't it?" She reaches for the pack of Pall Malls on the coffee table, packs one on her watch, lights it, blows smoke to one side with pursed lips, up and down to keep it out of Ruby's eyes. Then there is a long silence, suggesting neither think it is wonderful. They sit in emptiness—still, separate, alone—just the ringing of the ears and the removed sounds of a grandfather clock marking time, a train whistle down by the highway, a car motoring by, the scold of a blue jay, the buzz of a fly in the window. Finally Lena asks, "What do Carsten and Aksel have to do with it?" She laughs, "I mean, I know what Aksel has to do with it, but Carsten, how in the dickens Carsten?"

Ruby shifts on the ottoman, looks outside, then back. She locks her fingers and stretches her arms out in front of her, bending her fingers back, then rests her chin in a palm, elbow on her knee, legs crossed, bouncing a foot. "Remember I told you Dr. Meyer said something to Aksel about Carsten after I took Carsten in for his physical? How Carsten might be 'different' was how he put it. Aksel has never treated Carsten the same since. Not that he ever paid him attention like he does Anton."

"That dumb son of a bitch Dr. Meyer should never have said that. What the hell did he think he was doing?" Lena says, tapping her cigarette in the ashtray. She stands up and paces back and forth, arms crossed. She takes another drag. "You know, Ruby, as much as I think of Aksel, you have to set him straight. Carsten is his child, like it or not. Just because Meyer thinks Carsten is a sissy, or whatever you want to call it, does not mean a thing. You go home and tell Aksel how it is going to be. If you don't,

I will." Lena sits down and says, "Oh hell, Ruby, what're we going to do?"

"Why does it have to be this way anyway?" Ruby asks. "Why can't he just take Carsten with him? Like he does Anton, everywhere, every day. But never Carsten." Ruby takes a swig of her highball and screws up her face, having forgotten it was a highball instead of water. She sits the glass on the coffee table, sits back, crosses her arms, and stares out the picture window, watching the cars go by, children on the way home from school.

"Ruby ... have you ever noticed how men are really kind of gutless? Cowards?" Lena says in a low, even voice, as if saying something forbidden, known but unmentioned, seen but accommodated. She stares out the window like Ruby.

"What do you mean?" Ruby asks. "Aksel is hardly gutless. At least nobody sees him that way."

Lena muses, "It seems they are afraid of something. They want to be seen a certain way, or not be seen a certain way. I think they always have in mind what other men might think. Are they weak, are they soft? Chicken, in other words." Lena puts her hands in her armpits, flaps her elbows, and scurries around the room with her neck stuck out like a chicken running from a car. "Buk-buk-bugeeek! Ain't nobody in here but us chickens!"

Ruby drops her head, shakes it side to side, then comes up laughing. "Lena, you are something. Where do you come up with these ideas? Do you talk this way with Bert?"

Lena sits down across from Ruby, leans forward, and, eye to eye, says, "Listen, any man with balls would pick that kid up and say to the world, 'This kid is mine, and to hell with all of you!' But hell no—men think their boys have to hunt, ride horses, play football, fight, roughhouse, and all that stuff, and Aksel is no different. They are afraid to death their kid is going to make them look bad, less of a man, a man with a family that is less than they hoped for. Sometimes I wonder if they know what it means to be a man."

There is a long silence. Then Ruby asks, "What does it mean?"

Lena stands, stares outside, takes a deep breath, and slowly lets it out. Ruby looks up at her, waiting. "You know," Lena begins, "I've thought about this ever since my dad made my little brother box when he was just a tyke, bawling, bloody nose. Then when I was fifteen, I remember … Hell, I don't know. I think it means … getting beyond yourself, or getting beyond your fears someway. A man has to be damn strong, damn sure of himself to walk into a room full of men with a child that everyone knows doesn't measure up, or at least everyone thinks doesn't measure up. I hate to say it because it sounds so corny, but it's love, goddammit—can he love? Can a man show his love? Few can. You have to be able to be the child. You are one with that child come hell or high water." She looks down at Ruby, who is still seated on the footstool. "You know what I always wanted? I wanted my dad to say to me, with his voice, his eyes, his heart … just once … 'I love you simply because you are my daughter.' He needed to say it as much as I needed to hear it. Yes, I suppose he loved me, but I had to wonder. Was I a burden, in his way, just something that happened?"

"Aksel never saw it—love, that is—when he was growing up. He knows how to be proud, not how to love, care. He's a coyote trying to run with a pack of neighborhood dogs. And don't you ever say I said so," Ruby says as she begins to ready her personals to leave, to go pick up Carsten, to go home to fix supper. As she looks around to see if she has everything, she continues, "I got to go to college one year. We had to study Dante. I don't remember a thing except one line: 'Far from the goat shall be the grass.' That's how I feel right now." Satisfied she has everything, she sits gathered on the footstool. "Okeydoke, it's getting late. I gotta scram." Then she looks up at Lena. "You are the greatest."

Lena follows Ruby out to the curb and holds the door open as Ruby gets in. They have one more laugh, Lena imitating again the indignant pastor, and then Ruby drives off, Lena waving as she heads back inside.

Phew. That highball was strong. Ruby flicks her head. *Let's see ... What time is it anyway? Better get Carsten picked up; Gramma Beenie'll wonder where I am. That Lena, my, my. Don't need groceries, got gas.*

"Ohhh, I've got a pocketful of dreams ..." Ruby sings along to the radio—"I'm no millionaire, but ..."—and then goes back to her thoughts.

Aksel and Anton should be home soon. I've got to do something. Pregnant. And Aksel doesn't even know yet. Next time he has to take Carsten. Like Lena said, come hell or high water.

"How am I going to do this?" she says aloud and slaps the steering wheel. "If he gets mad, what'll I do?" She squirms back and forth in the seat and pulls herself up straight by the steering wheel as if she's made a decision. "I'll just take the kids and go to my sister's." She hits the brakes—"What was that?"—and then floorboards it. "Just a rabbit. Here come the trucks again. Take your half out of the middle, why don't you?"

God, I'm scared to death. What if he says no? Let's see—if he says no, then ... "Okay, Aksel, if you won't take Carsten, you can't take Anton either." *Oh my God, I can't even imagine. I feel like I could throw up.*

"Let's see ... what intersection is this?" She glances around. "Two more miles. I always forget."

What did she mean "beyond yourself"? She is so crazy sometimes. Men are scary.

"Wow, look at that." She slows. "A red-tailed hawk with something—a garter snake. Looook at that. It's keeping up with me, flying even, right beside me ... beautiful feathers, those wings, writhing, coiling, gliding, swooping. I'm the hawk. I'm the hawk—I see myself in the car. There's a lady in it. I'm watching the car and the hawk, the snake. I'm the snake, the sky, the sun ... Wow!"

She barrels on down the road, lost in thought. *For a moment it all stopped. My God! It was all one thing—I was one with that bird. Wow, murder! Woooooeee. Not since I was a kid underwater with that deep, terrifying hum that was everything. Now there's getting beyond yourself—not in my head, just out there. Who was that? It might've been me without all this stuff.*

And then she was back. "Okay ... I've got it now. 'Aksel, I love both of my children, and you are taking both or neither.' No, a different tone—'You should take both or neither.' Both or neither. Both."

*I could throw up. You know, this isn't even funny.
Aksel has no idea. There were so many kids in his family.
Kicked out when he was fifteen. His dad was mean,
mother always pregnant. Lucky if he was noticed. That
family was all about pride and money, who could win.*

"Love, you gotta be kidding me," she exclaims. "I'll
love you to pieces, Aksel. Ohhhhh, I got a pocketful
of dreams." She taps the brakes. "Where the hell is the
turnoff? Here we go. Carsten, my son, I'm here. It's you
and me against the world," Ruby announces as she gears
down and pulls into the Beenblossoms' farmyard.

Ruby raps on the screen door and walks on in at the
same time, as if a daughter coming home to visit, and is
about to let out an "Anyone home?" when Gramma Beenie
and Carsten appear from the living room, both aglow as
if they have something to share. Carsten hugs Ruby's legs
as she gabs with Gramma Beenie, and then he runs over
to the ear of corn and shelled kernels on the table. He sits
with legs swinging from the chair, eyes shiny, toying with
the corn, waiting for Mom to look.

Finally Ruby breaks from talking to Gramma Beenie
and looks over at Carsten with raised eyebrows to show
her gained attention, to acknowledge his excitement. "So
what have you two been doing, Carsten?"

"Warts," Carsten says as he looks to Gramma Beenie
for help.

"Warts?" exclaims Ruby, looking at Gramma Beenie,
then back at Carsten. "For sure he has some. The ones on
his knuckles crack and bleed sometimes. Been playing
with the frogs again I guess, eh, Carsten?" Ruby offers,
looking uncomfortable, like a mother found to have

missed something a mother should catch. "So what about those warts?" Ruby asks Carsten.

"You tell her, Gramma," Carsten says, gushing with excitement, unable to explain. Gramma Beenie pulls out a chair and starts to sit down across from Carsten, then motions to Ruby to take a seat before sitting herself.

"Well, he was sitting in there playing with the Kewpie dolls when I noticed the warts on his hands." Carsten looks at Ruby and then fidgets with the kernels of corn as Gramma Beenie continues, "So I told him to go out into the cornfield behind the barn and bring back an ear of corn and then to shell off a kernel for each wart on his hands." Gramma Beenie reaches over and pats Carsten's hands and smiles at him. "Then what did we do, Carsten?" she asks, and Carsten, too unsure, lays his head on his arm and gets a distant look on his face so as to ignore the question, avoid answering.

"Well, anyway, we got one of Grandpa's tobacco bags, and he put the counted kernels in there and tied the string. So then we went outside, east of the house here, and I blindfolded him."

Ruby looks from Gramma Beenie over at Carsten with a smile, knowing this had to be something different, exciting for Carsten, wanting to know his feelings. Carsten, uncomfortable with the attention, messes with the kernels on the table, avoiding eye contact.

"I turned—"

"Let me tell," Carsten finally says and jumps out of the chair.

"Okay, go ahead," Gramma Beenie says.

"She turned me around and around and then made

me face the east, and then I threw the bag," Carsten says, making a throwing motion. "Gramma says if the corn grows, the warts will go away. If it doesn't, they won't."

Ruby looks at Carsten with the expression of a sad clown, as if to say, *Hmm, what do ya think of that?* all the while thinking, *Carsten is going to want to tell this story to Anton and Aksel, and they won't be able to care less.*

The clock strikes seven. Aksel has an evening meeting in town and is preparing to leave, and Ruby has yet to find the moment, the courage. She can hear him in the bathroom, getting ready. She slowly dries the dishes, placing them as she does in the cupboard, quietly, one by one. She listens, waits for the right moment, heart pounding, still not sure what to say, how to say it, beyond thought, sensing separation, arrogance, and fear.

Carsten is in the living room listening to *Little Orphan Annie* on the radio. Anton is upstairs in his room. Aksel begins to move about with authority, putting on his jacket, fedora in hand, headed for the door. "Aksel," Ruby says in a voice that gives her away, that draws a line in the sand but begs for understanding, "in the morning I want you to take Carsten. You can't take one and not the other." In spite of her fear she holds her look, does not cower. Aksel, his hand on the doorknob, just ready to step outside, turns with slackened shoulders, head cocked to one side, a look of contempt on his face, a look of someone betrayed, of someone who counted on someone, of someone who thought he was doing right but it didn't count. He says nothing; just smiles a smirk that says, *Okay, if that is how it's going to be*, and walks out.

Ruby is startled awake by the sounds of a car door, the start of an engine, a car pulling out of the drive. In the early dawn darkness, the wind howling, sleet pelting the window, she gropes for Aksel on his side of the bed but feels only flat, cold blankets. *Never have we not slept together.* She flops back on her pillow overcome with panic and yet with an understanding of what she has done. *Carsten is different. I must do what mothers do. It's you and me, Carsten; it's you and me I guess.* She flips the quilts back, hustles into a housecoat, combs her hair with her fingers, and heads down the stairs.

As she swoops into the kitchen, a kitchen as cold as marble, dark, still, she is surprised to see Anton bundled up and in his buckle overshoes looking out the back-door window with his new Red Ryder BB gun in hand. Carsten is nowhere in sight. "Where's Carsten?" Ruby asks as she wraps her housecoat tighter and grabs the teakettle.

Anton doesn't answer, continues to look outside, then finally mumbles, "Outside." He opens the door, letting in a rush of cold air, and leaves. Still holding the teakettle, waiting for it to fill, Ruby can see Carsten out by the gate, under the mulberry tree, without a coat, the sleet angling down in the yard light. Anton walks slowly toward him and on through the gate. Carsten gets out of his way. She sees them say something to each other, Anton walking on toward the barn. Another exchange and Anton turns, takes aim, and shoots. Then he turns back toward the barn. Carsten does not wince, does not move; just looks after Anton for a long time with a look of want and hate.

Small Potatoes

August 1951

Queer. That's the word. That's the word I had to say to the cop. *Dick.* How do you say *dick* to a cop in front of your mom? Can still see 'em through the window. The cop with that big silver badge, some other guy in a suit with a bag-like thing, and my mom. All sitting at the kitchen table. Had to stand on my tiptoes to see in. Sent out there 'n' told to wait. The six o'clock whistle already blown when they showed up. Supper on the table ready to start.

Remember the neighbors' lights up and down the street coming on. No one was out there but me. Could hear the hay mills whining down by the tracks, 'bout all. Smell the alfalfa smoke from 'em. The houses grinned yellow grins like jack-o'-lanterns, like they knew something. Like a teacher or somebody's mom. Knew I was going to hell. Least that's what the Sunday school teacher tells us. Seemed like she might be right. It was starting to get dark. The cool creepies coming up out of the grass. I know something went from behind one tree to the other once. I know that.

Just me and Spud, my dog, out there. Spud because of all the potatoes around here. Wasn't so funny anymore. Then I remember smiling, petting Spud, sitting down in the grass, giving Spud a hug. Spud knew. Spud always knew. Spud knew and wasn't telling. Just me and Spud. But cops have a way of knowing. That's what Larry said. They can read your mind if you look 'em in the eye, he said. Larry had what my mom called a lazy eye. Couldn't tell if he was looking at you sometimes.

What was going on with Larry 'n' Cousin Kirby was the thing. What they telling? We were stealing potatoes, you know. Did the cops know about the cigarettes and the dime store? That's what I was thinking. The rest was small potatoes, my mom would say. How many people you know done these things when they were eight living in a small town in the middle of nowhere, eh? What're you laughing at?

So anyways, that morning we're down at the Dixie Inn, the café down by Highway 30. Me, Larry, and Cousin Kirby just fooling round, throwing rocks. Already been down to O'Conners five-and-dime on our way from the Sixth Street Market, where we cobbed some bubble gum. We were heading for the five-and-dime, walking down the alley, and saw Rasmussen drive by. The cop. We ducked into some bushes. Ran as hard as we could the other direction. He was always after us. Least we thought so.

Sure was fun thinking it. Sure 'nough, he passed the alley on the other end and went round the block, right where we ran to. We hightailed it through Mrs. Hanson's yard, split up. It felt like Rasmussen was right behind me. Thought I could hear his car gunning. Gave me a clutch in the neck, the willies. They say he can see around corners. Anyway that's what Larry says.

Met up again back at the little store panting and laughing. Then headed to the five-and-dime down the alleys again, looking out for Rasmussen. He'd be heading for coffee at Hap's café we were thinking. On our way we had a pissing contest. Sorry—shouldn't've used that word. Drew a line in the gravel. Had to stand behind it one at a time. Larry always won. He could put it out there about five feet. Kirby's nose was running like usual. Always had yellow snot creeping down his lip like a worm. He sucked it back in, knuckled it off. Goober, that's what we called 'im sometimes. Larry acted like he was going to puke and ran down the alley holding his ears. Kirby just laughed 'n' gave another suck.

Anyways, what was I saying? Yeah, you know I wouldn't be talking 'bout this if I wasn't wondering if that guy was out by now. Okay, so we headed for O'Conners, the five-and-dime. Starting to get hot out. The deal was you had to go in by yourself and steal as much as you could without getting caught. Mostly small stuff you could stick in your pocket. The worst place was the toy department. They kept their eye on you there. They could see you looking at the toys like you wanted 'em. Mrs. Paulsen would walk round behind you like a teacher. No good. Best to wander round till a customer came and Mrs.

Paulsen started talking to 'em. Then start snitching till you thought you had enough and then kind of whistle your way out while Mrs. Paulsen was still busy and head for the alley. You wanted to run, but you had to act like you were thinking and just looking around. Kind of a squint on your face, like you were looking for your parents.

The other two'd be back in the alley behind the dime store waiting. Then it'd be the next guy's turn. And every time we did it we just knew Rasmussen was cruising round the block. We'd hide in a space between buildings and count it out. Like maybe I'd cobbed two dollars and fifteen cents if you added the tags. That's what you had to beat to win. Next guy's turn. Best to go first. By the time the last guy went they were thinking something was up, or it sure seemed like it. Somehow they knew.

You know, I think Cousin Kirby won that day. He came out walking stiff legged. Had stuck a ten-dollar thing of some sort down his pant leg, showing through the hole in the knee. The dummy had a smile that wouldn't quit when he hobbled into the alley where we were. He knew he had a winner. Larry didn't even go in.

Then we did one of our best things and crawled up on the roof of the dime store and then ran around on the roofs of the buildings on that block, jumping from one to the other. The tar up there was gooey and warm from the sun. Larry was at the other end and yelled, "Rasmussen!" We scrambled like hell—oops—to get down and ran like crazy for a couple of blocks. Larry was laughing his guts out. I think he just yelled "Rasmussen" to make us get scared. We took off for the Dixie Inn.

So yeah, we were out in the parking lot at the Dixie,

throwing rocks at some crows watching us from some trees across the street, some trees over by the football field. Just then Larry said, "Look at that." He pointed to a truck in the lot with its back doors open. The guy was inside the Dixie. Kirby walked over to it like nobody's business, like no one was around, and next thing you know, he steps out with a carton of cigarettes. Philip Morris in the brown pack, our favorite. You think I'm kidding. Between the three of us we could always cob twenty cents from our parents—you know, cob it off the dresser or something. Go out to the feedlot, Armours, plunk the money in one of those red Canteen machines. Hell, we smoked like steam engines nearly every day. Never forget this. One day we were out in the chicken coop. Out dragging on some stogies. Larry said, "Watch this." He took a big drag, put his mouth on the side of the coop, and blew, blew hard. My God—sorry 'bout that— you should've seen the brown spot on that board. Nicotine, I guess. Made *me* wonder.

Hey, speaking of steam engines, getta load of this. There's a steam switch engine works this town. All day switching railroad cars here and there. 'Bout same time every day it'll take some cars out to Armours—you know, the feed yard. Anyways, the engineer was friends with Larry's dad, knew Larry. So we'd hide in the weeds 'long the tracks. We'd have handkerchiefs over our noses like robbers, our cap pistols drawn. Mounted on stick horses, we'd come riding outa them weeds when that thing came hissing down the tracks. They'd pull that black monster to a halt, hands up. That thing was scary. We'd climb aboard, and they'd let us ride out to the feed yard. Yeah, can you believe that shit? Oops, I mean, can you believe that?

So anyways, we hid the cigs in some weeds and headed for the potato sheds down by the tracks. You see, come end of summer they'd start digging potatoes. Ship 'em out on railcars. Two outfits were doing this every fall. Located side by side down by the tracks. So we'd go down there and get what they called thirds—you know, the small potatoes they'd throw away. We'd put 'em in a wagon and go house to house selling 'em. Ladies'd come to the door and make a big fuss over us. You know, three barefoot kids in bibs with holes in our knees pulling a wagon with a wheel gone. "Oh, how cute! Sure I'll buy some of those fine-looking potatoes." Can't make that sound they'd make, but you know, that high pitch like talking to babies or one a those little barky dogs or something. Anyways, they'd buy 'em, and we knew damned well—sorry 'bout that again—they didn't really wan' 'em. Fact, I went to one of those houses for something one time, and there was the potatoes all shriveled up on the porch. You could smell 'em going.

So here's the deal. That day we were hanging round this one potato shed to get some thirds. Larry had drifted off somewhere looking at things, how the potatoes are sorted and sacked. He came back excited. Motioned for us to huddle up. Some guy told him he'd get us some real potatoes. Some number ones. All we had to do was wait till the sheds shut down for the day. Then this guy'd meet one of us in back of the shed with a sack of number ones. Just come to his office. We were excited. So we waited all afternoon till quitting time, just throwing rocks, drinking

Nesbitt orange pop, watching what was going on. Could hardly wait.

So Larry said he'd go, beings how he was the oldest and biggest and all. Those spuds are heavy. Cousin Kirby and I, we waited cross the highway from the sheds. Waited for Larry to signal for us to come help. Well, we waited and waited. It was getting suppertime. Finally Cousin Kirby said he'd go find out what was up. So then I waited and waited. Both were gone.

Then here come Larry running toward me from the shed white as a newborn lamb, looking both ways for traffic. When he made it cross the highway, he shouted, "Queer, the guy's a queer!" He looked around. "Where's Kirby?" I told him Kirby'd gone to find him. We didn't know what to do.

Then there they were. Kirby and a big guy in those bibs railroaders wear, sides unbuttoned, no shirt. Brown and fat as a sow's belly. Walking toward us still on the other side of the highway. Traffic was making noise. Semis and a lot of cars. Larry was waving his arms, yelling at Kirby, "Get outa there!" Kirby kept yelling back, "Come on! He's got the potatoes!" Larry was getting mad because Kirby wouldn't hear 'im. Cousin Kirby was getting mad because we wouldn't get over there.

Then Larry cupped his hands and yelled, "He's queer! The guy's a queer!" Kirby held his ear, and it looked like he said, "What?" Larry yelled again, "C'mon! The guy's a queer!" This went on again and again. Kirby kept saying "Whaaat?" harder and harder.

Finally Kirby turned to the guy in bibs and said something, checked the traffic, and came jogging across the highway. "C'mon, you guys—he's got the spuds," Kirby said. When Larry told 'im, Kirby just shit—I mean, sorry, he looked funny. We ran. We ran for blocks. Headed for my house.

Sitting on the front porch, drinking grape Kool-Aid, we told the story again and again. Each time it got better. We hooted and howled and gulped Kool-Aid. We kept telling again and again how Larry would holler, then Kirby would yell back, "*Whaaat?*" Then Larry'd holler again. And then Kirby, "*WHAAAAT?*" Then Larry'd make that look Kirby got when we told 'im. I was rolling in the grass. Then Mom stepped around the corner. My sister had heard us talking through the screen door.

Well, Larry and Cousin Kirby had to go home, and I had to come in. Mom was on the phone, and it wasn't long before they showed up. You know, the guy in the suit and the cop. Yeah, it was Rasmussen. Larry got the strap when he got home. Mom had called his mom. And Cousin Kirby's folks, Uncle Eli and Aunt Phoebe, well, they were so damned happy—sorry, keep doing that— were so happy nothing happened they just let it go. I had to tell the whole story to Rasmussen and the suit guy. Use those words. Say what the guy in the bibs tried to do to Larry. Larry told me and Kirby on the way to my house after we stopped running.

This all sounds kinda funny, but I tell you, they put that guy in jail for a time, and he said he'd look us up when he got out. That's what he said at the trial. Larry told me. But then you know Larry. Mighta been another Rasmussen thing just to scare me and Kirby and make it fun.

That was three summers ago, and the other day I was home alone. The house seemed creepy, like it was talking. I think it was. Groans I hadn't heard before. And this car, the same old car kept going by the house. Again and again. It looked mean, like it was mad, just one eye and rattling like bones on that washboard road out front. It was getting dark out, and I wasn't sure when anyone would be home. So I turned on all the lights in the house and hid in the pantry, in the dark. Me and Spud. I remember thinking, *This ain't no small potatoes.* Anyway, I think that's what my mom was sayin' when I heard her say it to Aunt Phoebe on the phone that day. No sirree, no small potatoes.

Cousin Kirby was over the other day. Larry's down at the boys' training school in Kearney for something. Mom won't say. No sirree, no small potatoes. You hafta know who's lying. That's what Larry always said. Then he'd laugh ... yeah ... What's true—you know whadda mean?

Biggie Budd

A Sunday morning, 1954

The town was quiet, as if resting from a Saturday night of revelry, as if a carnival had been in town and then moved out in dead of night after the last ride. Only dogs and the town cop moved about, making their rounds in the purplish dark. Everyone else was still asleep. The streaks of daybreak in the east, a freight train rumbling through down by the river, the occasional chirp and trill of birds starting to stir, and the whine of the grinders and blowers at the hay mills down by the railroad tracks gave the town a forlorn feeling. You could hear coyotes yelping just outside of town, the last sounds of night. It was Sunday morning in July in a small town on the plains of Nebraska.

A mail-order small town out on the High Plains: huddled along some railroad tracks, sliced through by a highway running aside the rails, a main street, grain elevators, and a silver water tower. It had its amenities: a sand-greens golf course, a grass-strip airport, and a brand-new swimming pool with a high diving board. It had its hardware stores, jewelry shops and the like, and a café fit for a hardy breakfast at daybreak or Sunday dining after church. It had a honky-tonk Saturday-night bar, and churches on every corner. It had an area of new houses on the north edge of town where people drove Lincolns, Chryslers, and Cadillacs and a shanty town south of the tracks where people drove used Fords or walked. It had been settled by Danes and Germans. Migrant workers from south of the border came each year and worked the crops. Some stayed, and some were welcome—as long as they stayed in their place and were willing to endure taunts and icy looks, sport beatings if caught in the wrong place at the wrong time.

Twelve-year-old Frank Viig—in Levi's, Keds tennis shoes, and a white T-shirt—grabbed a piece of store-bought bread on his way through the kitchen, a kitchen still draped in darkness. He shouldered his way out the back door, reached over to give Tom, his cat, an ear tug, and then, holding the bread in his teeth, took a couple of running steps with his Schwinn bike, hopped on, and headed down the driveway. He flipped the canvas newspaper bags around the handlebars so they wouldn't get caught in the spokes. To keep Mom happy, he looked both ways for cars, then stood up to pump for speed as he took to the street and headed to the Union Pacific train station, where the *Omaha World-Herald* was dropped off for delivery.

Gangly, with outsized hands and feet, Frank was a boy showing signs of the man he would become: shoulders now wider than his hips, muscles that showed, hints of angular cheekbones, a Nordic nose poking out of a child's face, eyes that flashed like his grandmother Viig's. Dark. Serious. His physical prowess was that of his father. Otherwise, neither parent had left a mark, yet you could tell he was a Viig. The town waited to see if he had what it took, if he measured up to his father, Hans Viig, a very arresting man. A very arresting man who owned plenty of land, employed many of the workers in town with his various enterprises, and plunged into venture after venture—sometimes winning, sometimes losing. One year he bought up all the hay in the county and had it piled up ready to sell it, betting on the come, only to lose it all in a flood. Another year he let his alfalfa go to seed and sold it for a bundle. He did business with a handshake. His word was good enough.

Still sleepy, still dreamy, Frank rode no-hands in the darkness, munching on the bread he'd worked into a ball, enjoying the morning air, heavy with dew, pungent with the smell of alfalfa dust from the mills. It was a glorious morning. Through the monstrous elms and cottonwoods lurking over the street, blackened against the inked sky, the morning star shone in the east, and the waning crescent hung low to the southwest. Frank let out a long howl to answer the coyotes. Then, having finished the bread, he gripped the handlebars, pedaled hard, and steeled himself against the thought that once again his father's car had not been in the driveway when he'd left home. As Frank pedaled along, lost in thought, he recalled flying down to Wichita with his dad to get the new airplane at the Beechcraft factory. He'd gotten to meet Walter Beech.

"Hans, how did you get started?" Mr. Beech had asked his dad. They'd been standing with Mr. Beech in front of the first T-34 off the Beech Aircraft production line, a new military training plane for the navy. Mr. Beech had just finished explaining how the T-34 had been developed and how he'd gotten started in the aircraft business. Like Frank's dad, Mr. Beech moved about with ease in a tailored suit, shiny shoes, and a tie, like seen in magazines. His dad stood casually, a fist on his hip, brimmed hat was cocked to one side. Frank thought how great they looked, in awe of both of them.

Frank looked up at his dad to see what he was going to say. He had never heard him share his past. His dad's face flushed, as was his way when made uncomfortable. "Well, I suppose a lot like you, Walter. Raised on a farm. Got started farming myself and then developed several products using plastics. Bought my first Beechcraft as part of the business and then, as you know, got to know you when I became one of your first dealers. Thanks to you I've come to know Bill Odom and Bill Lear." The exchange caused Frank to recall getting to meet the famous Mr. Odom after his world record–breaking flight around the world in a single-engine plane named the *Waikiki Beech*.

"Well, if you're like me, then there's more to it than that," Mr. Beech said as he walked up to the T-34, sighting down the engine cowling as if to check something, then standing back, arms folded, proud of his latest creation. "My family made its way to Tennessee. How'd yours end up in Nebraska?" Mr. Beech asked as he squatted down on his heels to view the plane's underbelly.

Frank's dad looked down at Frank and smiled as if to apologize. "Well, my father, Jens, came to Nebraska when he was fifteen. He fled Bismarck's army, which had taken over part of Denmark. He ended up in Nebraska. His family knew some Danes there."

"Hans," Mr. Beech said as he stood up and walked back toward Frank and his dad, "if you are like me, you were damned glad to get off the farm." He smiled.

"I was the seventh of twelve children. Left home when I was fourteen."

"Why'd you leave?" Mr. Beech asked.

Then his dad shared something Frank had never imagined. "Jens, my father, buggy-whipped me for skinning the wrong horse." His dad gave him a look and smiled a wry smile as if embarrassed to be telling this in front of him and then turned back to Walter. "So I rode the rails to Chicago, worked a couple of years at Sears & Roebuck. Then went to Wyoming to be a skinner in the oil fields. Returned home at nineteen and worked as a farmhand until I could get started on my own."

"And look at us now," Mr. Beech said as he led the way off the production floor back to his office. "Successful entrepreneurs, making things happen. Hard to imagine, isn't it? Hans, I know you're accustomed to glamorous restaurants at Hollywood and Vine. But how about lunch with my wife, Olive, and me at the club and then step into our board of directors meeting after lunch before heading back. I want to introduce you to the board." Then he looked down at Frank. "And Frank too of course. You're going places, Hans. I want them to know you. What do you say?"

Frank and his dad had lunch, went to the board meeting, and then headed home.

On the flight back over Kansas, his dad piloting the new Bonanza that smelled like it was right out the box, Frank remembered watching his dad stare out the window at the earth moving below, deep in thought it seemed. He'd looked handsome, still crisply dressed as if it were the start of the day. But with his guard down and his mind apparently elsewhere, his face had been that of a tired and weary man. He'd seemed alone. Frank remembered turning and looking out his side, watching the section roads move under the wing, wondering about his dad.

Frank was thinking of that flight home, how his dad had seemed alone, weary, when blocks ahead, Frank spotted Biggie, the cop, stopped at the traffic light in the middle of town—the only stoplight in the county. Biggie slowly motored through the intersection, disappearing behind some buildings, making his rounds. All was still again except for a click with each crank of the pedals as Frank made his way to the train station, riding no-hands, picking at the wart on his knuckle, wondering where his father might be.

The lights of a car swung on him from behind, like a prison-tower beacon. Frank gripped the handlebars, pulled over to the side of the street, and casually glanced back over his shoulder to see who it might be but pedaled on, waiting for the car to pass. The car eased up alongside of him. It was Biggie Budd. Frank kept pedaling, then finally stopped when Biggie flashed his headlights. Astraddle his bike, elbows on the handlebars, Frank leaned over to look into the car window. Biggie, slouched back in his seat with his cop hat tipped back, car idling, blew a drag of smoke out the window, spit a piece of tobacco off the tip of his tongue, put his arm across the back of the seat, and then leaned across the seat to get a look at Frank.

"Didn't mean to scare ya," Biggie said in a voice scarred from years of smoking Old Golds. Then he laughed, coughed violently, hacked and spit out his window, and gently laughed again with low grunts.

Biggie was a huge and ugly man of some fifty years of age, a brawler in his day. He delighted in showing how a quarter could pass through his wedding ring. Well over six feet tall, big-boned and rangy, he was an imposing figure. Shoulders like an oxen yoke, hips so small his pants bagged as if about to fall to his ankles. No one messed with him. He never carried a gun, never wore his uniform except for that hat. He was hunched over in the shoulders, bent in the legs from fitting into spaces too small. He had to fold to get into his cop car or a booth at the local café, come coffee time. His pasty, loose-jowled, blue-lined face, accented with meaty lips and stained teeth, was saved by his smiley, robin's-egg-blue eyes. Biggie figured it was best to help the drunks home, warn the speeders, return loose pets to their owners, and give a warning to the parents of troublesome youth. The town paid him mileage to use his own car as a cruiser, a dark blue 1954 Mainline Ford. No siren, no flashing lights. Biggie Budd acted like he knew nothing but took note of people's whereabouts, habits, and contradictions. The town fathers thought him harmless, suitable for the job … and safe.

"I thought maybe it was my dad," Frank finally said. "Have you seen him?"

Biggie hesitated as if caught in a lie, straightened back up, shifted into low to gain time, hesitated again, apparently thinking. "Ya headed to the station?"

Frank said he was and was going to ask his question again but let it go. They shared a few takes on the beautiful morning. Then Biggie said he needed to get on with his rounds and pulled out. Frank took off again pedaling to the railroad station.

As Frank arrived at the station, the soot-covered, yellow caboose of a westbound freight train cleared the nearby railroad crossing. The squeals of dragging brakes, the lumber of heavy steel on steel, and the rumble of the ground were all fading away; the ding of the crossbar announced the freight's departure and the return to the morning quiet. Revealed on the other side of the tracks, as if a curtain had been pulled back on the opening scene, was Hans Viig's luxury Chrysler parked next to the curb at a rakish angle and Biggie Budd's cruiser pulling away the other direction with someone in the car with him.

Kickstand down, Frank walked from his bike, glancing back over at his dad's car before disappearing into the station. As Frank entered, the stationmaster—decked out in his green visor cap and navy vest, yellow pencil in his ear—was leaving the Authorized Personnel Only door to signal another freight going through from the west. The Hochtman boys, sons of a local doctor, juveniles ever on the verge of delinquency, were already inside folding their papers for easy tossing, preparing to make delivery. Always trailing the Hochtmans were their eighteen curs, none trained, all yipping, constantly fighting, but smiling ear to ear with the glee of running with the pack. Reluctantly, the stationmaster tolerated the dogs inside in the public area, though the Hochtmans knew he hated the animals. The Hochtmans had been poised for the moment the stationmaster stepped outside. As Frank entered, they each had two dogs by a hind leg, scurrying to toss them into the phone booth in the corner. As if catching chickens and throwing them into a crate for sale, they quickly caught and tossed dogs, one by one, into the booth and slammed the door. The dogs, at least ten of them, stacked in, wanting out, began to howl, fight, and squeal. The Hochtmans resumed their seats and continued to fold papers as if nothing unusual was happening ... and waited for the stationmaster to return.

Frank, stunned by the ruckus, watched by the door, assessing the situation, growing incensed and afraid—incensed about the dogs, afraid of the Hochtmans—yet he couldn't help but smirk. He dropped his newspaper bags and walked toward the phone booth, waiting to be challenged, not sure what he would do if he were.

As he opened the booth door to let the dogs out, the stationmaster burst from the back room, broom lifted, and began to beat Frank about the head and shoulders, yelling for him to get the hell out of the station. One freed short-legged, terrier-like hound snatched up a paper and started racing around the waiting area, ears flapping, daring anyone to try to take it away, the rest of the dogs chasing it, jumping up on the benches, over the top, and around the room again, barking and yelping out of confusion and excitement, resounding ever louder in the echoing vaulted room. The stationmaster went after the Hochtman boys, who headed for the door with shoulders hunched, arms over their heads, laughing and whooping it up. The barks and yelps turned to chaos and desperation, howls, squeals, and growls, as dogs scrambled between legs, some nipping at the stationmaster's heels before getting a swipe of the broom and scurrying out the door. Before Frank and the Hochtmans could gather themselves outside, the door opened, and out flew bundle after bundle of newspapers heaved with violence by the stationmaster as another thundering freight train steaming by from the west blasted its whistle, blotting out all sound. The ground shook, cinders and dirt swirled, Frank's bike fell over, dogs raced away around the corners of the station, papers were swooped up by the whirlwinds and dust devils kicked up by the freight, carried high into the air and all along the track for a quarter of a mile as car after car of the freight powered through until the caboose quietly followed them out of town and papers pirouetted and floated to the ground.

"Jeee-zuz-keee-*ryst*!" the older Hochtman let out, peering down the track as the dogs reappeared one by one from around the corners. The other Hochtman started picking up papers as if he might salvage the situation.

Frank finally broke from looking down the track and started to walk to his bike, but the older Hochtman stepped in front of him.

"Listen, shithead, you think you're hot goddamned

something because your ol' man's rich—big car, airplane, all that shit. I oughta kick your ass."

Frank set his jaw, heaved a slow breath, staring the older Hochtman hard between the eyes, and didn't move a muscle, thinking of his first punch if he had to throw one, prepared to go for the Adam's apple. After a long stare-down, the older Hochtman snorted and moved to go help his brother.

Frank got on his bike and headed for home, wondering how he was going to let his customers know what had happened, that they wouldn't be getting their Sunday paper. He'd stop off downtown for breakfast at Hap's café, then go home to sort out the newspaper mess and get ready for church. As he pedaled off, he glanced over and saw his dad's car had been moved.

Frank stepped into the town café, Hap's, with his hands behind him to keep the screen door from slapping shut and looked around for a seat at the counter, trying to be unnoticed, nodding good morning when he was. The café was a cacophony of sounds—waitresses yelling orders, the cook clinking a bell to let a waitress know an order was up, plates clanking, rolls of laughter from this group, hollers of greetings from another. Farmers were in for coffee after doing chores; fathers were in after dropping kids off for Sunday school, passing time before attending church or heading to the golf course.

As Frank passed to a seat, he acknowledged his elders with a proper salutation, as his father insisted. He slid onto a stool between a couple of farmers, regulars at the café, glanced around hoping to see his father, then locked eyes with Biggie Budd sitting across from him on the other side of the room, stirring his coffee. Biggie apparently had been watching him all the while, at the same time carrying on a conversation with the guy next to him.

Frank picked up the menu pushed to him by a harried waitress and decided on his usual eggs over easy and bacon, then looked around. The thick-necked farmer sitting to Frank's left had his back to Frank, facing the back of the café, and hadn't noticed him come in. Dressed in bibs, a sweat-stained, tattered straw hat tipped back, reeking of manure on his boots, he was expounding violently about something—the markets, the government, something—throwing his arms up to make a point, all the while dragging on a cigarette and blowing smoke up into the air between sentences, absentmindedly tapping the ashes on the floor before continuing on with the harangue.

Over the farmer's shoulder Frank could see a local attorney, the owner of the grain elevator, and someone from out of town Frank didn't know, all engaged in the conversation. Others at the edge of it tipped coffee and listened. All eyed Frank as he looked their way; all were friends or acquaintances of Hans Viig, except for the guy from out of town. Biggie Budd was watching, listening: listening as if he saw or heard nothing, all the while lending an ear to the guy sitting next to him.

The farmer went on, "The guy is in way over his head, I tell ya. He's down for the third time, and you can see the bubbles. He just keeps borrowing money, buying another goddamned airplane, heading off to sunny goddamned California, gone for weeks. Half the time his family doesn't even know where the hell he's at. He's drinkin' and carousin'. I say he's in trouble. I don't care how goddamned brilliant he is. This time the fox is not going to find a way out, and as far as I'm concerned, it's about goddamned time. He's a local kid who got into farming, made a bunch, then got to thinking he was big time. He's no goddamned better than you and me, I can tell ya."

"Who the hell you talkin' about?" the guy from out of town asked.

"Hans Viig. Do you know 'im?"

"No ... Heard of him; don't know him."

Some among the listeners averted their eyes and either uncrossed or crossed their legs, shifted in their seats, or smiled faintly like they had gas. Others sat as ramrod stiff and grim as a Baptist preacher seated among prostitutes. The farmer, who Frank now recognized as Jack Beasley, sensed something, and one of the grim-faced listeners raised his chin to signal he should look around to see who was sitting behind him. Jack hesitated, then put his palm on the counter and wheeled to his right, looking stiff-necked over his shoulder, and met Frank eye to eye just as the waitress slid a plate of eggs in front Frank. In the time it takes a hummingbird's wings to flutter, Frank thought of his father, whether he'd heard right, and what he should do. A coolness coursed through his limbs, and he swallowed hard and set his jaw, all the while keeping eye contact with Jack, who didn't move—nobody moved.

Then Frank stood up. He looked around, one by one, at the group of coffee drinkers gaping at him. Everyone else in the restaurant began to sense the tension and turned to look. Conversations died off. There was only the clanking of pans in the kitchen.

"Mr. Jensen ..." Frank addressed the eldest and most respected in the group, a close friend of Hans Viig. Then he choked on rage, stared for a moment, unable to speak without a cry in his voice. He turned and broke for the door, working his way past people turned to see what was happening, threw the screen door open, got on his bike, and headed west.

Later, a buddy of Frank's who happened to be there, told him how a buzz had set up throughout the restaurant as the onlookers all tried to find out what had happened, how Biggie Budd had excused himself from his conversation, awkwardly unwound from his stool and made his way out the front door, and, with hands on his hips, watched Frank disappear, apparently headed home.

Glum and distant, Frank held one side of the hymnal, his mother the other, as they stood and joined the congregation in the closing hymn "Shall We Gather at the River." They were in the third pew from the front, right side, where his mother—looking ever the part of Hans Viig's wife, ever that of a woman not herself—always sat, always leaving a space next to the aisle for her husband, who never attended. As the last refrain began, the part everyone was waiting for, they all began to sing with confidence and conviction. All joined in full throated and joyful, the sanctuary resounding with "Yes, we'll gather at the riiiiverrrr, the beautiful, the beautiful riiiiverrrr." Frank slipped the hymnal from his mother's hand, faintly smiling at her, and put it in the pew as he sang the part all knew by heart, gazing up at the minister, the choir, looking around at family and friends seated near him, lifted and carried by the final crescendo. "Gather with the saints at the riiiiverrrr that flows by the throne of Gaawwwwd."

The organ played on, repeating the refrain pianissimo. Members turned to greet one another, the choir filed out, children darted to get outside, and the preacher headed to the foyer to greet folks as they passed out the door, some hurrying home to check the roast, others to change clothes and get to the golf course. Frank and his mother waited for Hans's mother, who always sat in the front pew, to join them, then made their way together up the aisle in the shuffling crowd moving toward the door.

As Frank inched up the aisle, head down, thoughtful, listening to his mother and grandmother exchange time-honored pleasantries, he mulled over what had happened at Hap's café. How he should have defended his father, how his father would have expected him to do so. How he adored his father so very much, how his father was not what they said. How his father was everything he wanted to be, how if his father had walked in and heard Jack, he would have just smiled, and then he would have bought breakfast for everyone in the place just for the hell of it and stayed to drink coffee, even with Jack.

Jolted out of his musings by a hand on his arm, Frank turned to find his grandmother, tiny, dressed in black with a cameo broach and bird's-nest hat, looking up at him. She looked away, hesitated, dabbed the corners of her mouth with a flowered hankie, minced a couple of arthritic steps to get astride of him, and then looked back up with eyes like those of a blind dog.

With a voice cracked with age, raised as if Frank

were as deaf as she, she said, "Hans was always one of my favorites, Frank. Each was special, but Hans was different. You could tell he wasn't going to stay home. He was always looking for something. Hans knew there was something over the next hill. I wish God were in his life." Then she looked down, took a couple of steps to square herself with Frank, dabbed the corners of her mouth with the hankie again, and looked up at him. "He's never here, because he's too full of himself, won't sit with us hypocrites and pious sinners who are unwilling to ask questions. He hasn't found anything better, but then, maybe he's still looking."

She grabbed a hold of Frank's lapel. "We all look for a way to deal with the pain and fear, Frank, the feeling of being alone, separate. Ah, but you're too young to know. Most of us just accept what's in front of us. Hans is a seeker. He's out looking someplace else. He needs to look in his own heart."

Dora Viig held her look, tucking her hankie up a sleeve, turned and took a few halting steps up the aisle, then turned back just as Frank was stepping to follow her. "It's difficult to face yourself, Frank, and then admit there's something else, something bigger." She paused, craned to see if Frank's mother could hear her. "Frank, Hans isn't going to find it here," she said, pointing to the floor. "Neither will you. You're both pilgrims at heart; I can see it. Maybe if he loses it, he'll find it. You'll know he's found it when he looks at other people like they were God." Then she dropped off, put on her public face, and tottered up the aisle, beaming, engaging friends, waving with her fingers childlike at her great-grandchildren playing among the pews.

Just then his aunt, one of Hans's older sisters, an educated and striking woman, the wife of a local farmer and the congregation's self-appointed archangel whose glare could condemn an offender to hell, sidled up and slid her arm around his shoulder as they moved up the aisle.

"Couldn't help but overhear you talking to my mother, Frank. Just remember this about your father: when he was growing up, he needed some attention, didn't get it— dared to dream and share it, only to be dismissed. Your grandmother seems to forget all that. Hans has always reminded me of one of King Arthur's knights, ready to enter the forest at its darkest point to seek the Holy Grail, only to be ignored and told he was a fool and a sinner. Best I can tell, it has left him competitive and alone. So don't be too surprised that he seems wise yet reckless, bashful but daring. Distant. I love 'im to death, though, Frank." She gave his shoulder a squeeze, batted her eyes, and smiled at him as if to say, *And that's the Lord's truth*, then moved on up the aisle to converse with her mother and make sure the pastor was greeting people properly.

Frank took a deep breath and peered around for his mother, who was making small talk with folks as they made their way out. He joined her, and as they approached the pastor, the door, he was thinking of getting home and then off to the river to fish.

That afternoon the sun put a silver-white glare on everything. You couldn't look up. You had to shade your eyes and squint to look in the distance. The horizon seemed to shimmy as the heat boiled from the earth. Dogs sprawled under parked cars, panting, snapping at gnats. Window air conditioners hummed. The sun had everyone pinned down. No one was out.

Frank pedaled along on his bike, returning from an afternoon down at the river, a string of fish hanging from his handlebars. There was Biggie Budd parked in the shade of an elm near the train station with his door open, one foot out, smoking a cigarette, watching the Hochtman boys, apparently making sure they finished picking up all the papers along the tracks. Frank parked his bike in front of Biggie Budd's car, came around and sat down in the grass in front of Biggie, his elbows hooked around his knees, and nodded. Biggie smiled and flicked some ashes.

"Frank, you're a tough customer," Biggie said, tilting his head back, taking a long drag, all the while looking at Frank through eyes squinted to avoid the smoke. As he exhaled, he looked aside and flicked the cigarette with thumb and middle finger at something like he was scoring a basket. Then he turned back to Frank. "You think quite a bit of your dad, don't you?"

"Yes, sir. I want to be just like him."

"Just like 'im, eh?" Biggie said, looking down between his legs to let a ball of spit drop off his lower lip, stepping on a bug, twisting his shoe back and forth to squish it. "Tell ya what"—he looked back to check on the Hochtmans, then back around to Frank—"maybe you should think about bein' your own man … The world ain't perfect, ya know."

"Maybe." Frank wanted to ask what he meant, ask about his father's car.

After a silence—Biggie swatting at a fly, Frank staring, thinking—Frank rolled up on one knee like he was in the front row of a football team photo and pondered out loud in an absentminded way, "Who are you talking to when you think?"

Biggie hitched in the middle of a swing at a fly and eased his look over at Frank. Then his face broke to a smile. "My God, Frank, what the hell station you been listening to anyways? Del Rio, Texas? Wolfman Jack?"

Frank, still staring at the grass as if counting ants, monotoned, "Guess I'll head home and shoot some baskets." Then, shaking off the stupor, he announced, "I'll put him up against anybody," got up, got on his bike, and pedaled off. He looked back over his shoulder to check for traffic and could see Biggie watching him in the rearview mirror out his back window. Frank pedaled north, on his way home.

From a block away Frank could see his father's car in the driveway and was relieved, anxious to see him. Parked in front was Mr. Pedersen's car. Mr. Pedersen was a friend of his father. They often played in the same Sunday golf foursome and were probably having another round of beers after eighteen holes in the scorching sun. Frank put the kickstand down, untied the string of fish, and disappeared into the house, hoping to listen as his father and Mr. Pedersen swapped stories about the latest airplanes, products being developed, the marketing trip to Mexico, fads in Hollywood, and, of course, politics. Mr. Pedersen, a local farmer, would usually be shaking his head in doubt and amazement as Hans raved about progress and how to ride it.

Frank could hear Mr. Pedersen and his father in the living room. He put the fish in the kitchen sink, washed his hands quickly so as to not miss anything, and then moved through the dining room toward the living room, listening hard to catch the drift of the conversation, his heart quickening at the thought of being in the presence of his father and one of his cronies.

As Frank entered the room, Mr. Pedersen was saying, "Goddammit, Hans, you know I believe you. You and I know you didn't do it, so just forget it." Then he groped for something more to say. "Everyone knows you would never do such a thing. Why in the hell would anyone believe you would cheat at golf? I say to hell with Jack Beasley."

The shades were drawn. Frank's father sat in front of the fireplace on a straight-backed chair turned backward, his head resting on his arms on the back of it. The room reeked of beer. Empty bottles were sitting on a table and a partial six-pack was sitting on the floor next to Frank's father. Tag Pedersen was sitting on a footstool facing Hans as if tending to a boxer unable to answer the bell. Frank eased into the room, unsure what he had come upon, slack-jawed, eyes on his father, and took a seat to one side as quietly as possible, as if entering the room of someone gravely injured and dangerous.

Tag turned to Frank. "Jack Beasley accused him of not counting a stroke, Frank—he was in our foursome."

Hearing Frank's name, Hans raised his head slowly and gazed at Frank, trying to focus, head weaving. "What the hell's wrong with you? Haven't you ever seen a drunk before?" He continued to leer at Frank, his face contorted and flushed with contempt, with hate, with shame.

"Now, Hans ..." Tag started to say.

"Get the hell out of here if you don't like what you see," Hans said in a low, steady voice filled with self-loathing, continuing to stare at Frank with the eyes of a trapped and wounded animal, "if you're so damned ashamed." Then Hans tried to stand and screamed, "Just get the hell out of here!" He lunged out of his chair but was caught by Tag and pushed back down.

Keeping his eyes on Hans, Frank stood up in slow motion as if moving away from a coiled rattlesnake, glanced at Tag, then back to Hans. Hans gave way, lowered his eyes, breath heaving, gathering himself like that wounded animal, unwilling to accept defeat and death. Frank, caught between wanting to console and wanting to challenge, not daring to do either, just looked at his father. Then he slipped out the back door and headed south on his bike.

Each evening, before going off duty, as off duty as a cop in a one-cop town ever was, Biggie Budd checked the town public facilities. His last stop was the municipal airport just west of town, making sure the beacon was flashing, the landing lights on, the hangars secured. He turned off the highway, his headlights flooding the gravel road leading to the hangar area, and there ahead in front of Hans Viig's hangar were the silhouettes of a bike on its side and someone sitting on the ground leaned up against the door of the hangar. A jackrabbit darted in front of Biggie's car. The beacon flashed overhead. Biggie reached up, snapped on his spotlight, and swung it onto the figure, bugs swirling in the beam. It was Frank, his head turned, shading his eyes from the spotlight. Biggie pushed in the clutch, turned the spotlight and headlights off, and hesitated in the dark of his car. He took a deep breath, turned the engine off, and got out.

Biggie waited for his eyes to adjust to the dusk, then crunched through the gravel toward Frank. As he approached, Frank remained seated, staring ahead. The beacon flashed overhead, and Biggie could see Frank's glistening eyes and tear-stained cheeks. Frank looked away and wiped a cheek with the palm of his hand, holding his breath to keep from sobbing. Then he looked back, letting a breath out through his teeth.

Biggie pulled up the knees of his trousers, knelt down on one knee, and, with a grunt, swung down to sit beside Frank, his elbows on his knees. He said nothing. The beacon swung over them time and again. Crickets began tossing calls back and forth in time.

"I wasn't trying to get in," Frank finally said, in a voice caught somewhere between crying and explaining himself to the town cop. Some time passed; the beacon swung over them, reminding them of the silence.

"I know that … That isn't why I stopped," Biggie said after a bit. He slapped Frank on the knee without looking at him, with just the right bump to say, *I know*. Then he started the hunt to find his cigarettes, jiggled one up out of the pack, and pulled it out with his teeth.

"My father … Hans … is home drunk."

Biggie held his lighter to the cigarette, blew smoke up into the air, clicked the Ronson shut, and slipped it back into his shirt pocket, still blowing smoke out.

"Frank, I wish I knew what the hell to tell you. He's not the first dad to come home drunk, ya know."

"I think you know more."

Biggie looked down between his legs, rolled his cigarette in his fingers, and then looked over at Frank as the beacon flashed over, catching a glimpse of Frank staring off into the dark. Some time passed. Neither said a word. Then Frank stood up and began walking toward his bike, leaving Biggie sitting on the ground, awkwardly getting to his feet.

Before Frank could hop on his bike, Biggie, hitching his pants, flipping his cigarette, said, "Frank," then walked over to where Frank had one leg over the bike on the pedal, hands on the handlebars, looking down the gravel drive. "Cops always know more. Listen, this ain't going to be the last time you're going to be disappointed. Like I told ya, the world ain't perfect." Frank remained looking down the road; the beacon flashed.

"Why does he have to get drunk? Why can't he just be himself?"

Biggie put a hand on Frank's handlebars, the other on Frank's shoulder, looked down, hesitated, took a deep breath, held it, and let it out like he was blowing cigarette smoke, seemingly thinking.

"Your dad is different. People around here don't like that. They're going to make him pay if they can."

Neither moved. Nothing was said. The beacon swept overhead. Biggie jerked his head up to look at it, to gain time, and then looked off in the distance to track its path as it swept the countryside far into the distance. Then he looked back and with a plea in his voice said, "Frank, be like your dad. Dare to be different. Goddammit, you can make it. Most of us just settle in. Hell's fire, Frank, you can see things I'll never see, know things I'll never know. Who the hell would you rather be like—Hans … or Jack Beasley?" The beacon flashed overhead.

"No one."

Frank was still looking ahead. Then he pushed off, stood up on the first turn of the pedal to get through the gravel, and headed down the road toward home, howling, howling like a coyote. The beacon swept, catching Biggie, the cop, with his hands on his hips looking after Frank and Frank farther down the road with each sweep.

The White Ruana

October 1974

Hustling into the Omaha Symphony theater late, striding across the lobby, I tug each sleeve of my starched white shirt and straighten my tie. From the concert hall, there is the tapping of the conductor's baton and a dying babble. I open the door to the hall as if checking on sleeping children, praying it has been oiled recently, hoping not to be noticed. Hunched over like a thief in the night to acknowledge my faux pas, I take my seat; luckily it's at the end of the row. Then I settle in among the waft of perfumes, colognes, and aging bodies. I sit erect and formal as one does at such events, as if I had been properly on time all along.

Without moving my head, pretending to be enraptured by the first movement, I comb the audience to see if she is here—my sister, the one person who will understand what happened.

It has been meetings, court appearances, and late nights at the office since returning from Colombia. No chance to share, no chance to find the words. Not the words to explain the loss but the words to share what happened, what happened to *me*.

Yes, I explain to my sister at intermission, it was lost along with my luggage on the return flight. I found her holding forth in a ring of friends, looking gorgeous as usual, like a Jane Fonda in black with pearls, carrying on as if she herself were on stage.

She just looks at me, eye to eye. We both start to grin, more like a smirk; something our father gave us, a grin that says more than words.

"You don't seem very upset about it," she says in a coy way, moving away from the circle of friends, sitting down on a leather-covered bench against the wall, out of the way of milling patrons. She pats it for me to join her, a glass of wine in her other hand, and adjusts her skirt over her knee as I sit down.

Seated on the edge, my hands gripping the front of the bench, shoulders hunched as if about to stand, I hesitate and stare across the room, losing myself in that moment when the airline agent said my luggage was lost.

"You know, Sis, it was a strange thing. Normally I would have exploded and demanded to speak to the president of the company, making a scene. But I was as cool as a cucumber, almost serene."

"How could that be? That's not you," she says in a dismissive way, leaning to one side, putting the wineglass down on the floor beside the bench, casually glancing around to see if anyone has noticed.

How am I going to explain this? I think, turning to look at her.

"I already had what can't be put into words, and it can't be taken away," I finally say. "When I took that *ruana*, or poncho I guess most people would call it, out of the box and held it up, I experienced what I think they call artistic arrest. You are going to laugh and think I'm nuts, but I think I had a glimpse into"—I hesitate—"the divine."

I quickly look away, up and down the lobby, making sure no one has heard me, and then look back, smiling.

"Everything else just fell away. I think Shelley called it a fading spark shot from a fire. All opened, closed"—I snap my fingers—"that quick."

"Well, well, my little brother went on quite the trip," she says with a tease in her voice, placing her elbow on her crossed knee, chin on her thumb. Then she cocks her head to look at me, smiles, and puts her hand on my shoulder, giving it a squeeze.

"You haven't heard the half of it," I say as the bells sound, announcing the return to our seats.

"Give me a clue," she says, kicking off one of our favorite games, which requires a one-word response. She stands, flipping her hair back, then smooths her skirt.

I stand, hands on my hips, jacket pushed back, looking down, thinking. Then I look back at her. "Ego. No, wait, that's not it. Try 'death hyphen resurrection.' That's one word, isn't it?"

As we turn to take our seats, she pinches the slight

bulge of fat above my belt, a fond gesture which she knows I hate, and says, "Let's get a drink after this. I'll meet you here in the lobby."

The lights lower. Muffled conversations trail off. The baton is up. There is a long, suspended silence and then the haunting sounds of soft violins. As the music crescendos and begins to weave its spell, my mind wanders back to that moment when María turned to me and said what she did about the white sheep. *How do I share that with my sister? What words can explain it?* I wonder whether María felt it.

I smile wistfully and shift in my seat. Maybe María did. The *ruana* is sacrificed, but she sent me back with a boon, a gift. Then I'm lost in the music, remembering the trip as if in the moment, hoping to find the words. I recall the words of the physicist Schrödinger: "The show that is going on obviously acquires a meaning only with regard to the mind that contemplates it."

The Boeing 727 banks to land at Cali, the city not yet known for its drug lords but renowned the world over for its women and *ruanas*, both stunning. God! I wonder whatever happened to the *ruana* María promised me the last time I was here. The plane pitches and bucks in torrents of rain. The hydraulics whine to full flap, signaling touchdown at any moment. As it lowers, the landing gear thumps like a wing has just buckled. Some of us check for the nearest exit; others cross themselves.

This is the Colombia I remember, monstrous storms

at times, always plenty of adventure. Not having used my Spanish for two years, I feel a tinge of angst: How do I get downtown without getting ripped off by the cabdriver or dropped off at the *hospital* instead of my *hospedaje* in this strange and desperate place, late at night in a downpour?

Touchdown, rollout, nervous chatter; we act nonchalant again. Then through the terminal. It's like a ballpark postgame, empty except for a man with a lot of keys, a woman cleaning as if waiting to go home, a brown dog scouring for crumbs. I catch a cab to downtown.

"Hotel Continental, *por favor*," I instruct the driver from the back seat.

"*Sí, señor*," he confirms, and we go into the night.

I'm headed back to La Vega, a village of maybe a hundred people, a village of whitewashed, red-tile-roofed houses: houses constructed of mud, straw, and horse manure, strung along a mule trail through a pass high in the Andes south of Popayán. At that elevation, seven thousand feet, it's cold at night, chilly during the day; baked during the dry season, a mudhole during the rainy season. The place consists of a church, a school, a bar, the village office, and an open market on Saturday. But it's beautiful, with a feeling of the Swiss Alps, towering mountains, rivulets, patches of green pastures and corn plots. The poverty is staggering. Half the children born die before they're six years of age. In the early sixties, it was home for a couple of years when I worked with the Colombian government on a development project. Two years ago, in 1972, I returned for a visit anxious to see friends, yearning for the mysteries of La Vega. Always haunting me were the images of Julián and his wife, María:

indios surviving on last year's crop of coffee, maize, and coca, all raised on a few hectares on a mountain ridge above La Vega. Now I'm back again, to see how friends are doing, to enjoy Colombia. I'll ride out to where Julián and María live and find out why I never received the *ruana* María promised.

As the cab makes its way into Cali, I strike up a conversation with the driver, to see what he knows, dig for information. "What do you make of the guerilla activity?" I ask in rusty Spanish.

He looks at me in the rearview mirror, maybe not sure who I might be, then says, "*Quién sabe?*"

"I understand there is activity in Huila, near San Agustín," I continue, trying to prime the pump.

He looks at me in the rearview mirror, says nothing.

"I'm headed to Cauca, up to a village called La Vega where I once lived, across the mountains from San Agustín," I share.

"*Sí, señor,* where Tirofijo is, no?" he finally gives.

"That's my understanding," I say, recalling how Sureshot, nom de guerre for Manuel Marulanda, the leader of FARC, was operating in the region back when I lived in La Vega, making a mental note that he is still there.

"He is getting stronger it seems," the driver ventures.

Upon reaching the outskirts of Cali, I drop the conversation. The driver gives me another look in the rearview mirror and makes his way to the hotel.

Having dropped me off running for the door as if through a prairie hailstorm, the driver, in his sea-green 1952 DeSoto, waits to see that I make it and then pulls away from the hotel—windshield wipers pounding, differential grinding, the tailpipe blowing blue smoke.

The Hotel Continental used to be frequented by slick-haired salesmen, high-heeled prostitutes, and secret lovers. Nothing has changed, I note, as a giddy couple, glancing in all directions to see who may be watching, tries to hail my taxi as it pulls away. I check into the hotel. Cigarette burns in the carpet, cobwebs in the corner. I'm glad to have both feet on the ground. Glad to be back. I go have a beer at the corner bar, then slip into bed, wondering about fleas and tarantulas. Next morning it's off to Popayán, off to La Vega.

Early the next day—sun shining, parrots squawking, the streets already bustling—I catch the yellow-colored Línea Magdalena bus. Yellow Death we called it back then. Overloaded buses driven by Señor Macho passing on blind curves, smacking into other buses, plunging into a jungle gorge.

At Popayán, a remote colonial city encrusted with layers of whitewash, with cathedrals on every other block, I swing down off the Blue Bird–brand school bus, satchel in hand. For a moment it feels like game day, like I'm headed to the locker room to suit up. Then I'm back to making my way through hawkers of *chicharrones*, or fried pork skins; beggars for *una limosna*, or alms; and paperboys shouting, *"El Liberal! El Liberal! El Liberal!"* Off to the Hotel Monasterio for lunch, to get organized. Some time in Popayán renewing friendships, then on out to La Vega: La Vega where years ago I was saddling up a horse to go somewhere, tying up in front of the bar, meeting the mule train to get the mail, eating meat unrefrigerated for days on end, bathing every week or so, reading by candlelight, going to bed when the sun went down, getting up at the first glow of light. The thought of La Vega stirs my blood.

Making my way along Popayán's stone sidewalks, snug against whitewashed walls with openings into cathedrals, cafés, schools, and shops, I shoulder through giggling students in blue-and-white uniforms, solemn businessmen in suits, and barefoot *campesinos*, or peasants, in bowler hats and brown-toned *ruanas*. Living in La Vega was like an old western movie: Filemón, the schoolteacher, who took me under his wing and knew all there was to know about La Vega; Mauricio, the telegraph operator, who got tired of me asking whether I had received any messages; Señor Muñoz, the mayor, full of self-importance, empty as a spent cartridge; and the sister-prostitutes, who ran the only so-called café in town, where I frequently ate lunch.

I hope to see all of them again. But most of all I want to ride out to María and Julián's place, beyond La Vega, higher up in the Andes, about an hour on horseback. *Campesinos* living in a thatched-roof, dirt-floor hovel perched on the side of a mountain, scratching out an existence on a patch of rocks, growing maize, herding a few sheep, most of them black or brown, which I always found strange since the sheep back home were white.

As I walk the streets of Popayán, the massive, blinding-white walls and black iron gate of the former monastery, now a hotel, come into view, suggesting a plate of delicious grass-fed beef, garnished with asparagus, fried yucca, and fingers of mango, followed up with a dish of candied figs and gulps of Colombian coffee in a china cup. I make my way to the restaurant. The hostess, smoothing the white tablecloth, fussing with the red carnations adorning it, seats me. All eyes on the gringo: tall, dark, and different. She welcomes me to Popayán as I sit down, then asks where I'm from.

"Nebraska, a state in the middle of my country. You probably haven't heard of it," I say, spreading my napkin.

"I know Philadelphia," she says, pouring some water.

"How's that?"

"One of my sisters attended Penn, and I used to visit her," she says, setting the pitcher down.

"Really? I attended Penn also," I say. "I loved Philly."

"What do you do in Nebraska?" she asks, lighting a candle on the table.

"I'm an attorney," I respond, looking her in the face for the first time, our eyes meeting.

"And what brings you to Popayán? Business?" she asks, pushing her hair back.

"I lived here once, in La Vega. I'm on my way to visit friends," I say, waiting for her reaction.

"My God! La Vega. That is far and remote, where *los indios* live. I'd never go there," she says with less interest than before, and then she excuses herself to wait on some guests.

I smile to myself, and while I wait for someone to take my order, I wonder how it could take María two years to weave a *ruana*.

After having a scrumptious meal, I pay up and walk out into the glaring sun, wondering how to find the people I once knew here, wondering whether the bus for La Vega still leaves from that byzantine area of look-alike streets next to the open market. First I need to find a hotel to drop off my gear and spiff up a bit. Then I'll hit the streets. In a day or so it's off to La Vega.

Walking up the street, I feel my fear, no, awe of María. I will never forget her presence when she showed up at the field where Julián and I were planting corn. It was the first time I saw her: green-black teeth, some missing; a slow drool at the corner of her mouth from chewing coca leaves to ease the pain of hunger; greasy, pitch-black hair stringing down; head covered, like most *campesinas,* with a man's broad-brimmed, black hat pulled down on her forehead, shading her strong, mischievous eyes that looked like bullet holes in a snowbank; tired shoulders covered by a brown *ruana*; dirty, brown skirt down to her ankles; flattened bare feet; reeking an odor of cook-fire smoke and a sour body. All the marks of ever-hounding, bone-tired poverty. She moved about the field assessing what was going on with authority, with an aura of hardened but racked strength. I later saw her mean when cornered, confident when not afraid, driven by a savage will to survive. As she moved across the field that day, I watched her, making sure I didn't draw her wrath. She looked as homely yet as graceful as a mud hen crossing a slough. This woman is weaving me a *ruana.*

Finally I'm off to La Vega. The *campo* bus—basically church pews nailed on a truck covered with a platform for cargo, painted like a circus wagon, a plastic Jesus on the dashboard for passing on blind curves—is already full. After a night drinking a local hooch, *tragos de aguardiente*, with friends from my former time in

Colombia and let-me-get-the-next-round types, the prospect of riding all day with an electric-blue headache in an open, cramped bus grinding through the Andes Mountains on rough dirt roads looks bleak. I will get to Altamira about six or seven if all goes well. Then it's on foot the last ten miles up into the canyon, arriving by moonlight sometime around midnight.

As I find a place to squeeze in, I see familiar faces, nod *buenos días*, lean to shake hands, exchange glances: a big gringo stuffed in, feeling conspicuous among meek *campesinos* uniformed in brimmed hats and brown-toned *ruanas*.

We are off, family and friends, concubines and a priest, all waving, the matador driver blasting the horn to announce his entrance into the bullring of traffic. Me, eyes closed, ears ringing, stomach churning. It's going to be a day of numbing gear shifts, drops of passengers and cargo, jerks to a start, then stretches crawling at twenty-five miles per hour. Hopefully a Colombian version of Montezuma's revenge—more like Montezuma, Bolívar, and Calderón riding together—won't catch up with me.

While the bus meanders through the mountains, my mind wanders to my first year in La Vega when we were hit with a drought late in the growing season. Native corn does not mature for twelve months at that altitude, and that year it never put on an ear. I went to see don Lucio, thinking maybe I had a solution, at least for the next year: hybrid corn from the university experimental farm with a shorter growing season, fortified with fertilizer, that would produce a crop before the dreaded drought set in. That's how I met María and Julián. Their family could not survive the loss of another corn crop; they had to run a risk to survive. Don Lucio, a wizened *campesino*, who lived on a choice plot sided by two mountain brooks, enjoying the role of gentleman farmer and local *sabio*, or sage, was my best hope to gain cooperation for the experiment. With don Lucio's blessing, Julián and María, hoping to survive, ran the risk. They abandoned the ancient seed handed down over the centuries and planted that year's corn crop with seed out of a sack, spreading a sand-like powder with magical powers. It worked; the corn matured before the drought. Little did this young gringo understand they would have no money for more seed and fertilizer for the next crop. As the bus turns off the main Popayán-to-Pasto road to Altamira, the end of the road and the start of the long hike to La Vega, I shake my head. What a risk they took!

Around midnight, having just walked up from Altamira in the dark guided by moonlight, sodden from a bone-chilling drizzle, I knock on Filemón's darkened door with a crack of light around the edges, surprising him. He is still up playing the guitar, preparing his classes by candlelight, tinkering with one of his hobbies. I step in out of the mountain air, peeling off my soaked jacket, giving Filemón *un abrazo*, glad to be back.

After a coffee, the beans dried in the sun, roasted over a fire, ground by hand, and *un trago* or more of *aguardiente*, we trade stories: stories of days gone by, stories of what has happened, stories that make us laugh, stories that make us gaze into our cups, swirl the coffee around, then toss it down, and change the subject.

Filemón suddenly remembers that María brought the *ruana* down last Saturday, market day. As María and I agreed, when she was done weaving the *ruana*, she would bring it down to Filemón to send to me. He had it boxed to send, not expecting me to show up. As I take the box in hand to open it, I wonder why it has taken this long, though I've never doubted she would keep her promise.

As I open the box, I lose myself in thought, thinking of how two years ago I was here and saw Julián and María, living high in the Andes, huddled up and cold at night, hungry and life-tired by day.

We had become friends when I'd helped them plant the hybrid corn, poking a hole with a stick, dropping a couple of kernels, circling them with fertilizer, standing back looking at what we had done, feeling a great risk, hoping for the best. To celebrate we had shared a meal of coffee and yucca prepared over an open fire at their mud hut.

When I got to their place two years ago on my last visit, only María and the children were home. Julián had gone to work the patch of coffee down by Altamira. Having never been farther away from home than Altamira, she for sure had no idea where I had been the last number of years. She glanced up and greeted me as if I had been in La Vega all this time, as if I were just stopping by, as if she had expected me. She was on her knees at her loom made of tree limbs bound with twine, chewing coca leaves, laboring to create a *ruana* out of wool from her sheep, having sheared them and spun the wool into a brown thread, rolled onto a stick.

After the usual formal greetings, she left the loom to

offer me a cup of coffee, sweetened with *panela*, brown sugar homemade from sugarcane, and containing bits of dirt, shards of straw, and a fly or two, from sitting open as it cooled from boiling. She kneeled at the loom again, and we began an awkward conversation as she used crude sticks, the best flat ones she could find, to shuttle and tighten the weave.

The afternoon wore on, the sun warming us, the talk settling us, the weaving enchanting us. I felt free to ask María about her life, her story. Before long we were joshing each other, laughing and teasing, listening to each other, thinking and pondering: she always shyly, never looking me full in the face, as that would be inappropriate in her world. Once, she stopped her weaving, turned, and pointed across the way to Pancitará ridge, across the valley to the mountain on the other side, a steep mountain patched with pastures and plots bordered with hedgerows, dotted with huts, traversed by a continuous hedgerow, the mule trail, climbing to the summit. At the bottom, junglelike growth; at the top, the *páramo*, a cold, drizzly landscape shrouded in clouds. She pointed out the hut where she was born and raised, pausing, staring, as if to consider that little girl she once was and the hard journey since.

It was time for me to go back down the mountain, but watching María weave, it struck me how wonderful it would be to possess a *ruana* created by her hands, so I hinted at it.

"Sure," she said with a sly smirk, "but it is really going to cost you, you being so big."

We agreed on the pesos I was to pay. Half now and I

was to leave the rest with Filemón to give her when she came down with the *ruana*. Then she took a strand of thread and measured my long arms, still protesting in a teasing way about my size. She turned away as I was about to step into the saddle. Then she turned back.

"*Señor,*" she said.

"*Qué?*" I asked as I stepped into the stirrup.

"What color?"

I swung up into the saddle, looked down at the ground, and thought a moment. "*Blanco?*" I thought aloud, leaning over to slip my other foot into the stirrup. "*Sí,* white. I saw one once. I liked it," I said, straightening up.

She looked me full in the face with ancient eyes. "*Muy bien,*" she agreed with a slight smile and turned away.

I reined my horse out the gate, heading back down to La Vega, back home to the prairies of Nebraska.

Filemón, holding up another *trago* for me, brings me back as I finish opening the box. I gulp the drink down, then lift the *ruana* out, holding it up with one hand, eyeing it in the candlelight as it unfolds, bringing more light into the room. There is a long silence as I hold it up, continuing to eye it up and down.

"*Magnífico, no?*" Filemón finally utters reverently.

I am without words. I slowly sit down, spreading the *ruana* across my lap, gently running my fingers across it, as if trying to understand what has happened. Filemón watches me, smiling, apparently having had the same feeling when he first saw it. A white *ruana* so perfectly woven, where did it come from? As I caress it, I am taken by the heft, the exquisite weave, the smell of raw wool recently shorn, the subtle hues of the whiteness, its very presence.

At the break of dawn the next day, outfitted in chaps and packing a rain slicker in case it turns bad, on a sorrel borrowed from Filemón, I head out for Julián's place, catching the *camino* up to Calvario just outside of the village, after crossing the stream near don Lucio's. I figure it'll take an hour or so to get there, if the horse is fresh. I want to make sure I catch María and Julián before they head somewhere. The horse and I begin to climb, the *camino* in bad shape from the recent rains, the going a little rough, the footing slippery, causing the sorrel to labor and me to ready myself to step out of the saddle in case we go down. I let the reins, giving the horse his head to work; this is going to take longer than I thought. Anxious to get there, I push the sorrel, hoping not to miss them after coming all this way, especially María.

I swing down out of the saddle at the gate and flip the reins over the sorrel's neck. Looking him in the eye, I talk to him, pat him on his lathered shoulder as if to say, *Good job.* He raises his head, sets his ears up, looks wide-eyed over my shoulder, gives a low whinny, and shudders. I turn. There stands María, by the side of the house, looking at me. She is alone, the others working the field. I tie up. She invites me to take a seat on a wood bench, under the lean-to on the side of the house, looking out over the valley and mountains yonder. She sits down beside me, graceful, erect, hands folded over several ears of native corn in her lap, looking straight ahead, her bowler hat hiding her eyes. I lean back against the house wall, stretching my legs, wiggling my toes from being in the saddle, thinking of what to say. In the distance there is a roll of thunder: I need to be getting back soon to beat the rain, before night falls.

I ask how she has been, how the family is getting along, how the crops are doing. She shares that all is fine, *gracias a Dios*, not that she would say otherwise. I lean forward, forearms on my knees, poke around in the dirt with a stick. She sits the same—stoic, serene. We share small talk about this and that, with long, comfortable silences in between. Then, I tell her how wonderful I think the white *ruana* is, how much it means to me, how it will always be precious. Without embarrassing her, I try to catch the look on her face.

She heaves a sigh, smiles faintly, and looks down, still erect and stoic. To break the awkward tension from feelings shared, with a wry smile in my voice, I tease her, as we can with each other, about it taking so long.

"The *ruana* is *muy bonita*, but two years! *Por qué?* Why? What took so long?" I ask, ending in a respectful voice.

She turns to me, pauses, then demurely says, "*Señor,* you said you wanted a white *ruana*. I have only one white sheep." She turns back.

All quiets; nothing moves. The stick motionless in my hand, I turn my head and look at her. I want to take her hand. I look at her as long as I dare, then drop the stick, sit up straight, as if in church, a hand on each knee. Thunder rolls long and deep up the narrow valley. The hushing sound of advancing rain moves in around us, settling to a steady, gentle murmur. María, slowly chewing coca, looks out over the valley, then begins husking the ears of corn.

Walkie-Talkie

August 1984

Sweat trickles down my armpits as I lie naked, hands behind my head. I'm thinking about the woman next to me, the sticky heat, and some goddamned barking dog. Neither of us can sleep. It's two in the morning on a suffocating August night in an attic bedroom; the room seems sealed. Both of us must get to work in the morning; she to her bar restaurant, me to my law office in the next town. We're both still young and foolish. Finally, after an hour of avoiding each other's clammy body, after tossing and turning, after pretending to be asleep, we give up and talk. The only sound in all of the night is the damned barking dog somewhere across town. A town the size of the proverbial wide spot in the road, snuggled around a grain elevator, alongside a single railroad track snaking through the clay hills of south-central Nebraska, far from anything but corn and cattle.

The constant bark reminds me, for some reason, of the village idiot where I grew up in a two-bank, three-gas-station town the distance of a couple of songs on the radio down the road from here. And that is how we thought of him back then—the village idiot. I chuckle and tell Sybil about Walkie-Talkie.

"You know how mean kids can be," I say. "This guy was huge, wore bib overalls, big straw hat, walked fast everywhere he went, and, I swear, looked just like Baby Huey. He worked at one of the hay mills—used a picnic basket for his lunch pail. I can still see that green, fake-weave picnic basket with the wood handles. We called him Walkie-Talkie."

"Why Walkie-Talkie?" Sybil giggles, rolling up on an elbow, tracing a finger around my sweaty face.

"Everywhere he went, he talked out loud, constantly," I say as if in thought, staring at the ceiling.

I take a deep breath and hold it, pondering the memory, thinking about my father, remembering the smell of the flowers. It's quiet as a stone outside, just crickets chirping, the damned dog barking.

"What's mean about that?" Sybil teases.

"Well, we used to see him on the street on the way home from school. He would be on his way to the night shift at the mill, and we'd go walk behind him to listen. Then we'd yell, 'Hey, Walkie-Talkie, what's the other guy saying?' You know, like he was talking to someone on a walkie-talkie. It was right after World War II, so we knew about walkie-talkies, those two-way radios they used. Then we'd laugh and run, making sure no grown-ups saw us."

Sybil stops twirling her finger, looks me in the eye, then kisses me on the cheek as if to say, *I see.* I look at her, and we both smile faintly, knowingly, and then she rolls her eyes and flops back giggling as the barking dog breaks the spell. We laugh like kids.

"Do you care if I share something with you?" I ask as I sit up, leaning back against the headboard.

"Sure, go for it. I'm Tonto; you're Lone Ranger. I've got you covered," Sybil shoots back.

"Well, when I was in the second grade, one night my dad and I went uptown for supper. Mom must have been busy or something. I remember this so clearly; we went to Elston's Café down on Highway 30," I say, sitting up straighter, as Sybil sits up yoga style, facing me.

"Now the thing you have to know is my dad was an important man in town, very successful, very respected. Always dressed like straight out of *GQ*. Handsome, as in Clark Gable. I was so proud of him. And I was at that age when it is important to be accepted, free from taunts, safe from scorn. Believe me—my dad gave me all the cover I needed."

I glance at the window, gathering myself, and then look back at Sybil with a smirk; the damned dog, absolutely the only sound in town, is still carrying on. She shakes her fist at the open window in mock anger at the dog, then turns back to me with a smile.

"As we pulled up to the café, I see the cars of two of my classmates' families. As luck would have it, two of my girlfriends are there dining with their parents—Mary Jo and Sara. Class sweeties. I was madly in love with both of them, and I was there with my dad, and I was proud, excited," I say.

"We walk in the door, my girlfriends' families sitting in the booths waving to us, my dad acknowledging them, and guess who is sitting at the counter. Walkie-Talkie," I end, drawing out the last two words as if in disbelief.

"I remember thinking, *God, I hope my dad sits a long way from him.* Would you believe, my dad goes over, sits right down beside him, and carries on a conversation with him during the entire meal. I'm thinking, *What will my girlfriends think? How embarrassing. They'll tell everybody at school. I'm done!*" I shout at the end.

Sybil squeals with laughter, giving me a shove like, *Get out of here!* I stare at my feet smiling, relishing the memory, amazed at those old feelings. We acknowledge the barking dog with a glance.

I clear my throat, shifting my weight, and continue, "Years later, when I was fifteen, my dad was killed in an airplane accident. I was home alone one day before the funeral, devastated. In shock, I suppose, just going through the motions, hoping it was just a nightmare. The doorbell rang. I went to the door, and there stood Walkie-Talkie—with a pot of flowers for my mother. He had walked a mile out to the nursery, then back to town, and then a mile out to our house carrying that pot of flowers."

There is a long silence.

"I can still smell the flowers."

Neither of us says a thing for a long time; just stare, thinking.

"Years later I learned Donald Short suffered from shell

shock from being in the Bataan Death March on Luzon. Yeah, kids can be mean," I offer up, eyes glistening.

Sybil takes both of my hands, looking me full in the face. "Your dad was special," she says, knowing I don't dare try to speak. The dog is carrying on in the distance.

Something catches our attention: the sound of an electric garage door opening and a car backing out. We freeze and listen as it stops, then accelerates at each stop sign, making its way across town.

Then there is the crack of a gunshot.

The car makes its way back across town, slows to pull into a drive. The garage door closes.

It is totally quiet.

"Now *that* was real western," Sybil says, with eyes the size of saucers.

Rasmussen

September 1985

Oh my God … So you want to know what happened clear back then.

Well, I have a busy day, so I'm glad you're willing to tag along. I'll try to explain. First I've got to drop these clothes off at the cleaners. I'll just pull in here and be back in a moment. Hang on.

But while you wait, know this: I can tell by the color of the sky things are brewing. And I can smell fall in the air. Can't you? The colors, the trees are just gorgeous. Okay, so this'll take just a sec. I'll leave the car on; it's chilly out here. Back in a sec. And please, just call me Sadie, okay?

So anyway, thanks for waiting. Took 'em foreeeever. Is there anyone behind me? The old dude ahead of me was paying his bill. Fumbled around with his pennies. You're chuckling. No, I said *pennnnies*. You're nasty, gal. He was counting them out one at a time, dropping 'em on the floor. My God, just slap some bills down, take the change, and get the hell out of the way.

By the way, I like your purse. Where'd you get that? ... Garage sale. You gotta be kidding. Cute. And I love that black jacket you have on. Really brings out your blonde hair. Nice ... This? Oh, it's a sweater I picked up in Peru. I just love the colors, don't you? ... Well, thank you. Brings out *my* gray, but that's okay.

Is there anyone coming that way? ... Okay, we're off. So let me get this straight. Would you crack your window a bit? So you're with the paper, the *World-Herald*, Omaha. Right? ... So what's the deal? Why the interest in something that happened thirty years ago? My God, my dad's been dead twenty years or better ... Excuse me, just a sec—I've got to go by the food pantry. That okay? ... Look at that sky, would you? See how those clouds are swirling? That means something, I'm telling you—that means something. I've seen it before.

I see, I see. No, go ahead and take notes. No problem here. Soooo what with so-called innocent people being let out these days, they're taking a look at the potato-shed guy. Sorry, that's how folks around here think of it. The potato-shed guy. Is that the thing? ... I see. Well, that's interesting. Let me pull in here, and then we'll talk about it. Got a bunch of canned food we never get around to using. Thought I'd drop it off here. I'll pull right in between theeeese two cars. There. Come on in. You should see this. Hold it a sec before you get out. Get this. Because of the packing plant being in the county and all, we've got all sorts moving in—Mexicans, Somalis, Sudanese, you name it. Come on in; you'll see what I mean. Watch the curb. You won't believe the stories. Let's go in and see where they want the stuff unloaded. The door's over here ... Really? Well, I doubt that's the case here. I'll bet it's those just off the boat or still wet from wading the river who use it most.

Thanks for getting the door. Okay. Let's hop in and head for the church. See what I mean? Did you get a load of that? Whoa. Wait a minute, before you get in, did you see it? Three crows on the sidewalk in front of my Fleetwood, and then they took off when we stepped out. Did you see that? Swirling clouds the color of doom and three crows pecking around my Cad. Are you sure you're not the Wicked Witch of the East? Just kidding. But hey, it's not even ten o'clock yet, and I'm seeing signs. But I'm always seeing signs, which reminds me: don't let me forget to tell you what happened the day after the grain elevator thing.

Okay. Here's the church. Isn't that stained glass something? But go ahead; I'm listening. But before you do, did you notice all the Mexican kids out on the streets, the signs in Spanish? Tell me things haven't changed. So yes, go ahead ... You want to know whether the potato-shed guy was convicted unfairly. I'm not sure I understand. Why do you think that? And before you get into it, let's take these clothes in. If you don't mind, grab a box. My knees are killing me.

Wow, the wind has really whipped up. We'll go in this side door and leave them in the basement. Watch your step, and don't let the wind catch the door. We've got a clothing drive going. Many of these folks have no winter coats, gloves, that sort of thing.

So yeah, just set it down over there. My land, this place smells musty. Listen, just in case the pastor shows up, not a word about the potato-shed guy, okay? This pastor is in from California and off the charts when it comes to liberal ideas. We'll never get out of here if he gets started. Hey, thanks.

So I think that's it. Let's head on over to Gisela's house. What a darling *she* is. You wait and see. She cleans my house every Tuesday, just a darling. Not like most of 'em. She's so kind and does a great job. Never complains, does just what I tell her, and s*oooo* cheap. Always make sure I tip her a little. She thinks I look like Joan Jett. Can you believe that?

Okay, back in the saddle again. Crack that window if you would. We'll head on over to Gisela's house. She doesn't have a phone, and I need to know when she's coming over. Listen, before I try to answer your question— what was the question again? ...

So okay, was the trial fair? Well you know, I was just in high school then. What I know is mostly from what my dad said, the chief of police—Rasmussen, as all the kids called him. And I guess that's why you're talking to me, right? ...

Hey, listen, before we get into this, you need to know what it's like around here. My grandfather was in the Klan during the twenties and thirties—anti-Catholic. Guess there weren't any N*eee*groes around to string up, so they raised hell with the Catholics. And so now let me tell you about the elevator deal. Wait a minute. Maybe I should pull over while I relate this, before we get to Gisela's house. My God, the glare off my hood. Can't see a damn thing. She's just a couple of blocks ahead.

So here's the deal, just to give you an idea. My God, look at those clouds. You would think it was Gethsemane all over again. So anyway, we have a celebration every fall. You know, the usual. You probably noticed the grain elevator when you came into town—the big, white tubes a block high with our town name plastered on them. Can see it for miles. Every town out this way seems to have one. Corn cathedrals we call 'em. In Europe they have church steeples; here we have grain elevators. And in the fall we get pagan and drink and dance. The harvest is in.

Excuse me. Look over there. See that bright-pink house trimmed in red with five cars around it, one that runs. That's where we lived when I was growing up. Look at it. You can guess who lives in it now. By the way, do you need something to drink? ... We'll stop by the little store on Eighth, or maybe Gisela will have something. You okay, dear? ... Some coffee, some black coffee that will eat a spoon, that's what *I* need.

So, fine, one year, not so long ago—God, when was that? Eighty-one, maybe eighty-two. Doesn't matter. The dance was going on down on Main Street. The booze was flowing; the band was thumping. People were dancing with their heads thrown back, their hearts in the stars, smiles as wide as the river out south. Why, people were dancing with folks they weren't going to speak to or even acknowledge the next day ... Next day? Hell, *ever*. The barn doors had been flung open, and the horses were bolting for the other end of the pasture, you could say.

Now keep in mind, this town was settled by Germans. I mean everyone around here is a Kraut and related. You can't say anything mean, because sure as hell you're talking to someone's cousin. Half this town has an overbite, I swear to you. What are you giggling about? It's true. I swear. Now get this. That night at the stroke of midnight there was the damnedest ripping noise from over at the elevator just a block from the dance. It sounded like the flapping of a million birds, the unloading of a herd of buffalo down a boardwalk. Everyone stopped in their tracks and looked—everyone except for those too drunk to think something strange had happened. The band died with a single last whack of the snare drum. There down the whole side of the elevator was a fifty-by-hundred-yard canvas portrait of Adolf Hitler. In dead silence everyone just shit. Now get a hold on yourself, gal. This is for real. Then off from behind the elevator you could hear some cars start up, heading out of town to the south, honking their horns, hooting and hollering. No one ever figured out how they got that thing up there.

It turns out it was a bunch from down south of 18, Highway 18, a dirt road really. I tell you, once you get down there, it starts to feel like Missouri. You can hear the strumming of banjos. You drive around down there, and you can hear target practicing. And believe me, it's not ka-pow, ka-pow; it's rat-a-tat-tat, rat-a-tat-tat. You know what I mean? No way is this Elmer Fudd after a bunny wabbit, okay?

Well, the next day there was hell to pay. I swear the moon came up in the west, clocks ran backwards, because there was a tremor. I know. I felt it. The river ran red with

sumac leaves. God was not happy. These were signs. Do
you believe in signs? ... Well, you should, because they
happen all the time and most folks miss them. I learned
about signs the time I thought I was pregnant, still in
high school, scared to death. I prayed and prayed to just
let me off this time and I'd never have sex again ... *ever*.
A couple of days later there was some kind of eclipse,
moon, sun, something. Anyway, I had my period. Am I
telling you too much? You're giggling again. Now, I'm
not making this stuff up. Anyway, I didn't have sex again
for a month.

Well, enough of that stuff. You get the idea. You
know, sitting here looking over at our old house gets me
to thinking about Rasmussen, Dad. I think I know what
you're after. He was a good cop. Had to keep the big shots
happy. Get 'em home when they were drunk, not pick
up their kids when they drove underage, did wheelies.
Had to break up fights down at the bars, put friends in
jail. Never made much money. Had to kiss ass and take a
punch, possibly even a slug someday. And people wonder
why such folks get bitter, why they want to take it out on
someone, get even some way, keep from being a nobody.
When you know you're not going anywhere but backwards
and you have to kowtow to a bunch of former classmates
born sucking silver spoons, well, you can get bitter. But
he was a good cop, and he always had a smile. He was
true blue—the honest cop. And now you want to know if
the potato-shed guy was framed. That Mexican. Right? ...

Wait a minute. Your position is that he buckled. He
caved in to the bigwigs in town who wanted the guy
fried. Is that your point? What makes you think that? ...

douglas k german

Okay, okay, yeah, I know. You're just being a reporter. But who in the hell is saying this? Where are you getting your information? ... So you're going to hang your hat on what some coffee slurpers down at the Dew Drop Inn are batting their gums about ... I can see where this is going ... Yeah, yeah, you're just getting started, but I can see where this is headed ... Where am I going? ... Let's head back to my house, back to your car. I'll catch Gisela some other time ...

Yes, you're right. That was the question even back then. *Hey!* Goddamned drivers, get that crate of a car out of the way. Go back home if you can't drive. Yeah, it's been the question ever since. Why did they send someone up based on a kid's story? That was the question. Especially when the kid had a reputation: a reputation for telling tales, imagining things, dreaming things up. It's a good question. But I get the feeling you're trying to bring this down on my dad someway ... Oh, well, *I* think that's what you're doing.

There's your car; we're here. Now get out.

South of 18

October 2017

The way I met Calhoun, I was sitting in the bar, the only bar we have in town. At the time, I had my heels hooked on a stool talking to Jack, sipping a red beer. Jack glanced over my shoulder toward the door, and I felt a draft on my neck as someone walked in. I could hear the jingle of spurs. I remember thinking, *Who in the hell wears spurs these days?*

Jack chinned a howdy to whoever it was. The guy strode in and took a stool to my right. I turned to him as he sat down, turned so as to include—didn't say anything; just offered to buy him a drink. I figured he was a friend of Jack's. He thumbed his hat back, motioned for his regular, and grunted a "Thanks." A black, sweat-stained cowboy hat rolled just so, I should add. Greasy locks hanging out.

I could smell cow shit. The guy wiped some chew drool off his gray-stubbled chin: a chin scarred, scarred with a purple line from the lip down. Dressed in black from cowboy boots to western-cut shirt to neck kerchief, he was. Hard not to notice.

The barkeep slid down a whiskey of some sort. The guy tipped it back, slammed it down.

He bellowed, "*Who are we?*"

The other two in the bar, down at the other end, twirled around and eyed down at us. We all waited for the answer. The guy stared ahead as if to let the question sink in, straight-backed, hands out and open like *he* was waiting for the answer.

Then he whispered, "We are our stories."

Dead silence. And I couldn't help but think as I stared at him in the mirror behind the back bar, behind all the bottles, *That is pretty goddamned profound.* It was Calhoun. Before the evening was out, I learned Jack had known Calhoun since high school. And that is where *this* story begins.

A couple of weeks later I happened upon Jack again. He had been tied up hauling corn to the elevator and hadn't been around much. I was in about the same boat working some ground up. It was beer time, and as I got out of my pickup in front of the bar, Jack drew up. He motioned me over to his pickup and rolled down the window. Told me to get in. His dog, Farm Dog—that's right, Farm Dog, an Australian shepherd—raced around in the back of the pickup happy to see me. I gave her a tussle on the snout as I got in.

Jack was covered with corn dust. Two wet eyes peered

out of an ashen face, his Pioneer seed-corn cap and red plaid shirt grayed, blue jeans ripped at the knees, smeared with grime. When he spoke, his white teeth and red mouth were like an open wound, like a person doing blackface. I guess I wasn't much better, having just finished some field work. We were a pair to draw to as my mother would say.

"Wanna show you something," Jack mumbled as he pulled out. The whine of the fans circulating air at the grain elevator across the street eased to a hum as Jack rolled up his window. You could feel fall was in the air.

I suggested if we were going very far we should grab a six-pack or two. So Jack pulled around the block, and I ran in to grab a couple. Just as I stepped out of the bar, the six o'clock whistle let go up at the fire hall, and Farm Dog howled, joining the rounds of protesting dogs across the village. The shrill siren and eerie baying knifed a nerve, made me hunch my shoulders as I got back into Jack's new Ford 150, so new it still had In Transit signs. And then the whistle died down; the howling gave out. We took off, rumbled across the railroad tracks, cracked a couple of Bud Lights, and headed south.

Nothing was said. We headed down East Canyon Road. Jack got over damned near into the ditch for an eighteen-wheeler coming into town to dump corn. It was someone in a Diamond T. All we could see of him was a ball cap and a toothy, white grin peering out the cab, the dust so thick we couldn't see a thing for a quarter mile after we passed.

"Goddammit," Jack sputtered as the dust cleared. "Look at that pit in my windshield from that asshole. He owes me a keg of beer. The son of a bitch."

"That pit was there before," I intoned and tipped my beer, looking out the side to ignore his stare.

I was wondering where we were headed. But I thought, *Hey, we're beered up, so we're good.* Then again, it was a little strange Jack headed south out of town; he farms north. I wasn't going to give him the satisfaction of asking. *Just wait and see,* I was thinking. *Let Jack play out his little drama, his mysterious "Wanna show you something."* I was game and wasn't going to flinch. He wanted me to ask. I know Jack.

After a swig of beer I choked out, "Ever wonder why they call these canyons, canyons?"

Jack looked over at me like I'd asked why dirt was called dirt. "What the hell you mean?" he managed as he swerved to miss a pheasant scurrying across the road.

The speedometer read seventy I noticed. We were clipping along on a winding gravel road most folks took at forty. That was another thing about Jack. He wanted his passengers nervous, saying something about his driving. I wasn't going to say a word and took a long swig.

"Well, look around," I went on. "Does this look like the Rocky Mountains to you? An outsider would giggle themselves silly. *Canyons?* Hell, this is a holler, a dell, a glen, at best a valley."

"A dell, eh?" Jack said. He took a swig and looked around at the hills we were passing through as if to measure what I'd said. "A *dell* you say," he said absently, like he was trying to speak French. "Like the farmer in the *dell*, right?" He chuckled deep to let me know he thought I was full of shit. He took another swig.

We both went quiet. Sliding through curve after curve,

leaping across narrow bridge after narrow bridge, with the fence posts on both sides of the road whipping past in a blur, we made our way south. I noticed Jack taking looks out at the pastures, the hills. It made me do the same. The question seemed to have him thinking, had both of us thinking. I cracked a couple more beers with my good hand, the one with all its fingers, and handed one to Jack.

I was wondering if he was seeing what I was seeing. Some folks look at these hills and wonder how many cow-calf pairs could be run. That's Jack. I saw scenes to paint, walks to take. But like Jack, I always checked the fences, how the guy handled fencing over that creek, up over that hill. Were the wires tight, the posts in a straight line?

As we were rumbling along, I was composing in my mind a scene to paint of the plum bushes with hues the color of eggplant, the black-trunked ash trees, the dark green cedars, and the blue-stem grasses with traces of browns and reds, the catsteps on the hillsides, a crow's nest high in a cottonwood. A bobcat or a mountain lion was what I was hoping to see up one of the draws we passed. I turned back and gulped a couple o' swallows of still-crispy beer and let out an *awhhhh* and a belch.

We were coming up on the Henniker place, which meant we were coming up on Highway 18, a graveled east-west highway across the middle of barren hill country. It starts to get a little strange down in here. But Jack was bent on something. I still wasn't going to say anything. I just took a swig and looked around at the changing landscape, wondering what was up. Jack and I farm north of town where things are a little different. The land is flat, the soil black-rich, irrigated.

Jack pulled up to the stop sign, checked both ways, and crossed 18, and we headed on south. He held his hand out for another beer. I crushed his empty, tossed it on the floorboard, and got another one for myself and him. I looked around. Now it was going to get interesting.

"Ever wonder how these folks make it down here, farming these hogbacks?" I was referring to the way they farmed the ridges of the hills, pastured the canyons. Most of it was dry land, made a crop about every third year. The other years the crop just dried up and shriveled away. It was a hard way to make a go of it. Jack didn't say anything; just nursed his beer and barreled on down the road. I harrumphed a chuckle to myself; folks from these parts spend the winters out in the barn straightening nails trying to save a buck.

The farmsteads got fewer and fewer. The roads back into most of them were two dirt wheel tracks leading to the top of a hill where an unpainted house, a sagging barn, and a tilted windmill stood. The corrals looked like a string of fallen sticks. Maybe a lone car was parked out front, the only thing with paint in the whole scene. Most of the places seemed abandoned, even the cars. Made me wonder who the hell lived up in those places. Meth came to mind.

We passed a sign tacked to a fence post: Gilchrist for President. It didn't ring a bell for me. I turned to see Jack's reaction. When I turned back, there was another sign on a post: Spics, Niggers & Liberals Shot on Sight. I squirmed back and forth in my seat and leaned forward a bit to get a better look at what was coming up. Jack did the same, pulling himself up by the steering wheel, looking around. It was just more country road, but it seemed different.

"Okay," Jack eased out as he slowed down and peered around, "this is Calhoun country." He hesitated, surveying around as we idled along almost at a walking pace. Then he said, "Get my forty-five out from under the seat here." He slapped the seat. "See if the clip is full, loaded, and make sure it's on safe." Then he looked at me. "And don't blow my goddamned foot off doing it." Jack knew I wasn't much for guns.

We eased along the road for a mile or so, not saying anything, just looking around. I got a couple more beers out, checked the sack for how many we had left. Jack pulled himself up and took the beer without taking his gaze off the tops of the ridges on both sides. He cleared his throat and jerked the bill of his cap to one side like some kid on TV. With Jack this always meant something was up. He broke the silence. "So before we get to his place, let me explain a thing or two about what we're getting into."

I don't remember everything Jack mentioned at that point. Wasn't paying all that much attention really. Those signs we passed had me thinking, looking for others. But apparently Calhoun had been an outstanding student in high school. Honor roll, that kind of thing. A hellion for sure, but smart. Brought up right. Parents real Bible-thumpers, I guess. But anyway, when he got out, he'd started a business of some kind. Something his dad had been involved in. He'd turned it into something big, according to Jack. Something big. He'd been a success. Then things had gone to hell, and he'd been working cattle for his neighbors pretty much ever since, holed up in these hills. Well, to say the least, turned out there was more to the story than I first took to heart.

We crossed over a small wooden bridge that rattled and clapped as we passed over it. Jack pulled to a halt. "The drive to his place is just up ahead." He chinned for me to look on down the road. Jack popped open his door and had one foot out when he turned back and said, "Let's put Farm Dog up front with us. Calhoun has a bunch of throat-ripping junkyard dogs." We both took the opportunity to take a piss.

Then Jack got Farm Dog out of the back and up front with us. She promptly knocked Jack's beer off the dash, so happy to be up front. We cleaned things up best we could. I cracked another beer for Jack, and we headed for the turn up to Calhoun's place.

"Ever notice how people who have failed at some point in their lives get into conspiracy theories?" Jack—his cap still turned sideways, his face still ashen with corn dust—looked over at me as he finished the question. He was about to turn in at the drive. I didn't say anything. But I remember thinking, *I hope there are two ways out of here.*

We began the climb to the top of the hill, up to Calhoun's farmyard. Like the other places we'd seen from the road, it was junked up. The barn was leaning. Fireweeds head tall had taken over the place. The chicken coop and hog barn, as best we could see them, were ghosts of what they once were. Nothing was painted. Abandoned farm equipment was sitting around here and there where it was last parked and never used again. Everything stuck up out of the sea of fireweeds like debris floating with the tide. We passed a corral with horses in it as we pulled in. Sure enough, a couple of German shepherds came bounding out of nowhere, jumping up on the doors of the pickup, snarling at the windows. Farm Dog went bullshit. Jack swung around and parked in front of the house. The pickup was nosed downhill toward the corral of horses, the road out of there.

The house? It was a strange sight. I leaned forward to get a good look at it. It was in perfect condition, just like it must have looked when it was first built back in the twenties. It just didn't have any paint. It was eerie. There was the rose trellis, the wooden swing on the screened-in porch. Perfect. Just no paint. Beyond the porch was probably a living room leading to a dining room on into a kitchen and most likely some bedrooms tucked along the sides and then a basement and a back door. Most of us grew up in something like this.

But let me get to what happened next. It was dusk, and there was a light on in the house. The German shepherds continued to raise hell. We were sitting there with our beers in hand looking at the house. Jack, with his cap still cocked to one side, had laid on the horn a couple of times hoping Calhoun was home and would come out. Just as I was about to take a sip of beer, there was the goddamnedest bang on the window on my side. Farm Dog jumped. I spilled my beer all down my front. Jack whipped around and grabbed for the pistol. There stood Calhoun outside the pickup window without a smile on his face and with an AK-47 in his hand. Well ... after all was said and done, after Calhoun recognized Jack, he penned the dogs, and we were invited to come inside.

Now, I don't mean to exaggerate, but I might as well have been sitting at Nazi headquarters in Normandy on D-day. The room was red and black with swastika flags and other regime regalia. Framed photos of Jesus and President Trump hung on the wall. I couldn't believe I was sitting there. The place reeked of weed. Calhoun— outfitted all in black, cowboy hat pulled down tight—had taken what looked to be his favorite chair, which had the hint of a throne about it, and Jack and I were seated like schoolboys answering to the principal.

For sure this guy was holed up ... alone, angry. Scared even.

It looked like he was in hell to me.

We all had a beer. It was awkward.

"So ... what's going on?" Jack finally mustered and raised his beer as if to say, *Here's to ya.* His cap was on straight now.

Calhoun stared at Jack through a set of John Lennon sunglasses, rapping his fingernails on the arm of his chair. He had the look of someone who knows he has a victim. "Same ol' shit, Jack," Calhoun allowed, "just a different day." Like a rattlesnake, he was eyeing Jack, waiting for his move.

I just kept my nose out of it. Jack and Calhoun touched on one thing and then another. You know, the weather, how the folks at home are, ever see so-and-so—that sort of thing. I gandered around the room best I could without Calhoun catching me doing it. I could tell Calhoun knew we were in over our heads and should never have shown up. He was just waiting, like a dog waiting for the prey to get up, start to run.

It didn't take long for Jack to pick up that Calhoun was waiting. There was going to be a price to pay to get out of there. I could tell, and I could tell Jack could tell. If Jack thought he could have got away with it, he'd have turned his cap to the side. That was Jack. But then there was Calhoun.

And Jack began to run. "Well, I guess we might as well head back. Got chores to do yet," he said. The prey got up out of his chair. I stood up more than ready to go. Calhoun just sat there looking at us. Then he got up, and we all three moved toward the door, Jack and me making small talk, thanking him for the beer, that kind of thing. Calhoun didn't say a thing; just followed us out the door.

I didn't think much of it at the time. But looking back, it should have raised the hair on the back of my neck. As we reached Jack's pickup, Calhoun made his way around us and ended up between us and the pickup, like he was going to open the door for Jack to get in. I was about to go around to the other side to get in. Calhoun turned back to us as he reached the pickup. Then he just leaned against the door, an arm slung inside the open window, and stared at us. Farm Dog raced around inside, sniffing Calhoun's neck, wagging her tail. Calhoun paid no never mind, as we say in these parts. Jack and I stood there, each with a thumb hooked in our belts, wondering what was up. But I think we both knew the price was about to be paid.

"You guys think you know the way back to town?" Calhoun eased out.

Neither of us said a thing. I knew no matter what we said it wasn't going to do any good. I just didn't know what was next.

"Then start walking," Calhoun said as he slipped the pickup out of gear and gave it a shove to get it started rolling down the hill toward the horse corral. Jack made a go for the pickup to try to stop it, but Calhoun stepped in his way. Jack and I watched the pickup, Farm Dog dashing around inside. Calhoun never took his eyes off of us; just waited for the crash.

The pickup went through the corral boards, down into a hole, and smashed into the water tank for the horses sitting just inside the corral. There was a helluva noise, as you can imagine. Boards flew; water from the tank shot in the air. The horses bucked to the other end of the corral. Then it went quiet. Dust drifted from the scene in a cloud. I couldn't see Farm Dog. The back end of the pickup stuck out of the corral, the front end down in the hole, the hood about where the corral boards used to cross. I glanced over at Calhoun. He was still just looking at us: looking at us with a slight smile; hadn't moved a muscle.

And then the damnedest thing. One of the horses came trotting back and nosed around the wreck. The next we knew, it began to hoof it over the hood of the pickup and out of the corral. And sure as hell, the other horses began to follow. The racket, the clamoring, like horses stumbling and sliding out of a barn on fire, made Calhoun break his stare to see what the hell was happening. Jack made a dash for the pickup. I followed and got there just as the last horse stumbled across the hood and was out. Farm Dog stuck her head out the open window, I remember.

As Jack and I stood there looking after the horses as they stampeded down the road out, Calhoun sauntered up. We all three watched the horses disappear over the hill into the dusk of night. And then we heard the first one cross the wooden bridge, then another, then another, then another, then another.

"How many did you get?" Calhoun asked.

"Five," Jack said.

"That's what I got," Calhoun confirmed.

"So they're all heading in the same direction," Jack offered.

I turned to look at the two, thinking, *Jesus Christ, we've got this situation on our hands, and these two yahoos are carrying on like they're sorting cattle, getting a head count.*

Jack broke from the trance of looking after the horses and began to clear the boards away from the pickup. He got in and cranked it over. It ran. He was able to back it out and get it up on the road. Then he got out to check the damage. We all three stood in silence looking at the hood. It was smashed clear in. It looked like a big bowl with all kinds of scrapes and dents. The fenders were all hacked up also. Jack didn't say anything; just motioned for me to get in. Calhoun stepped back a bit, and we pulled out, Farm Dog happy to see us.

We were about out of the yard when Jack skidded to a stop and backed up. He was looking at Calhoun's John Deere tractor parked by the road. He fished for the pistol and brought it up. He came down on the right rear tire and squeezed off a round. It echoed up and down the canyons. Then he did the same on the other rear tire. The air hissed; the tire fluid squirted. Jack turned his cap sideways and pulled out.

We weren't far down the road, headed back north,

when we came upon the horses. They were still cantering along the road, tails up, ears pricked, snorting. Jack eased his way around them, making sure he didn't run them into the fences. Then he stuck his hand out for a beer.

Jack leaned my way a bit while looking down the road. "Did I mention he doesn't much like people showing up at his place?" I was looking at him when he said it. He looked over at me. Big grin, hat sideways, eyes shining from the dash lights. It was pitch dark out, there was lightning in the west, and we still had chores to do when we got home. I took a swig of my beer and thought back on what Calhoun had said that time in the bar. We are our stories.

The End

As Tolstoy suggested, the best stories are about someone going on a journey of some kind, or a stranger coming to town. So . . . go on a journey, ask 'Who am I? Invite in the stranger – greet yourself coming into town, coming home.

—dkg